Praise for the inspiring books of Sophy Burnham

A Book of Angels

"Like all good books, it exceeds the subject and illuminates the tough, tiring, and sometimes miraculous business of living, where angels sometimes help out. . . . The visible and invisible dance with each other continually and as far as angels are concerned, now you see them, now you don't. *A Book of Angels* gives us a lovely, sustained glimpse."

—*Chicago Tribune*

"Lovely . . . *A Book of Angels* is the apt addition to any home in which wonder and joy are still appreciated. . . . An inspiring and touching book."
—*Cape Cod Times*

Revelations

"A passionate book . . . [Burnham] is a gorgeous writer. . . . She deserves a readership as broad as her talent."

—*Los Angeles Times*

"A hauntingly unsentimental and tragic love story."
—*The Washington Post Book World*

Also by Sophy Burnham:

Nonfiction:
THE ART CROWD
THE LANDED GENTRY
A BOOK OF ANGELS*
ANGEL LETTERS*

Fiction:
BUCCANEER
THE DOGWALKER
REVELATIONS*

Plays:
PENELOPE
THE STUDY
A WARRIOR
THE WITCH'S TALE

*Published by Ballantine Books

THE PRESIDENT'S ANGEL

Sophy Burnham

IVY BOOKS • NEW YORK

Ivy Books
Published by Ballantine Books
Copyright © 1993 by Sophy Burnham

Library of Congress Catalog Card Number: 93-16459

ISBN 0-8041-1285-1

Manufactured in the United States of America

First Hardcover Edition: September 1993
First Mass Market Edition: December 1994

10 9 8 7 6 5 4 3 2 1

INTRODUCTION

The President's Angel is the third and last of my angel cycle. Three books, two nonfiction and one novel, were written in a rush of creativity, all on some aspect of the spiritual journey. All three are about the visits of angels and what happens when you've seen an angel.

This last little novel came to me both instantly—all in a flash—and slowly, painfully, crawling from my pen, my flesh. And yet, as with the two nonfiction angel books, the writing was also accomplished in a transport of joy.

It was in the mid-eighties, I forget what year. The world was gearing up for Star Wars and anxiety ran high. According to one poll, one-half of the American men under thirty believed an all-out nuclear war would occur within a decade.

A good friend in New York called to urge me to take to the barricades with the other artists in her group. "We're all marching this weekend against the XYZ Military Installation. You HAVE to come."

"Oh, Ellie," I said. "I don't do that."

But I felt miserable about my inability to engage, and lying on my bed one afternoon I began to think about the fragile state of the world, and my own inadequacy. I had just finished reading a biography of Padre Pio, the Italian priest who died in Apulia in 1964. He was blessed with stigmata, the bleeding hands of Christ. He performed miracles, could bilocate, and is considered by some a saint. It was said that whoever prays to Padre Pio will immediately receive that prayer. Lying on my bed that afternoon, I prayed to him and God.

"I wish I could do something," I prayed wordlessly. "I wish I knew something. I wish that I had some insight into what is happening, and since I cannot demonstrate with the others, that I could be of some help to this poor pretty little suffering world. . . ." Prayers like that, wordless yearnings.

A sentence came into my head. "It was on the 695th night of his reign that the President saw the angel." And another: "He awoke from a light and fitful sleep to see the form balancing on the end of his bed." By then I had reached for the pen by my bed and I was writing furiously. The words were pouring out. I wrote in a kind of delirium for possibly fifteen minutes, came to the end of the chapter, and stopped cold. Nothing. The Muse had fled.

But I read the chapter over in wonderment, feeling its power and knowing that I wanted to know the end of the story, what happened to the President—and knowing too that I had perhaps been given an answer to my prayer.

Then began the slow construction of the tale, and the sense of gnawing at the story. Sometimes it came pouring out of me, thundering from where I had no idea, and sometimes I would wait for days, straining to hear the etheric words that did not come. I don't mean to sound magical about it. All writers believe their words are sometimes gifts of the Muse, and at the same time the writer works and works, preparing the soil to produce this fruit.

People familiar with my work will recognize two images in this novel. That of the picnic you can find in my novel, *Revelations*, and the story of the black dog and prayer in *Angel Letters*. But apart from those two images, this work is entirely its own. Indeed this fact of constantly breaking new ground presents a problem for the publisher—and also for an audience perhaps—that I, the writer, will not be contained by any form, but write novels, nonfiction books, plays, essays, journalism, children's stories ... heedless of the marketplace that slots the writer to a certain form and place and subject and style.

But all my work is similar in having a spiritual as

well as a physical dimension, in its hope and joy and love for the courage and idealism of humankind.

Writers have their own jokes. For those people happy enough to have had a classical education, I have hidden a little treasure in this book. It is a game of fox-and-hare, a literary Trivial Pursuit, in which the reader may come across a phrase—five words, a line—that rings a bell of recognition. Shakespeare, Gerald Manley Hopkins, John Cheever, Dante, Arthur Miller, Milton, Rilke, Voltaire . . . See who you can find. There are eighteen such little gold nuggets buried in the text, unmarked. Their presence is of no importance whatsoever; the text makes perfect sense without their recognition. You can read the book straight through and never notice one, and you should feel neither victory nor defeat either way; but for me they act as private, friendly signs, like the smile of a secret lover flashed across a crowded room. So I give them to the literary hound, an extra puzzle to sniff out, or to the casual reader as a kind of valentine.

When I finished *The President's Angel*, it was met (as were all the other works in this cycle) by my agent's loud disinterest. Time passed. I had grown discouraged by then. My work was too philosophical. Or too unusual. It didn't fall into any category or genre by which an agent or publisher could sell the stuff.

No publisher, therefore, saw this little novel, although several of my writing colleagues read, edited, and gave wise comments.

Time passed, and now the book appears in print, and to my surprise I find that many of the things I thought outlandish when writing them, like peace between enemies, have come about.

Is it possible that there are more things, Horatio, than this world dreams of? Are there angels—principalities, powers, virtues, and dominions—governing our nations and political affairs? Mystics say that we should have no doubts.

1

It was on the 695th night of his reign that the President saw the angel. He awoke from a light and fitful sleep to see the form balancing on the end of his bed. The President no longer slept with the First Lady by then. She said she could stand the snoring but not the moans. He had moved into the East Bedroom, where he found an unexpected benefit: Each morning through the east window, he could watch dawn break open the shell of night. Somehow that had become important to him.

The President had no trouble dropping off to sleep. He finished work around ten P.M. (and he counted state dinners as work these days, he who had always been ready to dance and talk till one). By eleven he retired to his rooms, to read or brood. Twice recently he found himself desperately holding on to Anne. "How was your day? What did you think of the Ambassador's new young wife?" He didn't want to face another pile of memos placed on the nightstand for him to consider before he slept. But the President was in bondage to the White House, to rules, to procedures, and to computer printouts. Sometimes his eyes were too tired to focus at night. He asked Frank to read the memos aloud while he lay in bed, eyes closed. They usually brought bad news. The economy recovering . . . means rising inflation. . . . The Other Party is preparing an attack; your advisors recommend . . . This is the latest news of war in the Middle East, war in Central America, war in Ireland, war in Africa, war in Asia, war in the Far East. . . . Good night, Mr. President. Sleep well.

Each night he fell into a pool of sleep, where he stayed suspended dreamlessly for as long as three hours at a time, before jerking awake, alert as an outlaw. A night-light on the bedside table permitted him to find his glasses. He would read mystery novels, plowing through one paperback after another until, eyes blurring with fatigue, he'd fall asleep again, but this time fitfully and fighting off the dreams.

Therefore it was not unusual for the President to awaken with a start at four A.M.

He regarded the specter without surprise. It was white. It was luminous. It seemed to have a human form, and yet no definition at the edges of its shape, as if, being made of light, it blurred away. And yet it had a face. An aureole of hair. And clothing of some sort of light. He—or was it she? The President could not tell its gender. It balanced on one foot playfully, then hopped onto the other in a kind of minuet. Seeing the President watching, it stopped and seemed to melt until both feet settled on the footboard, then slipped on past, or possibly through the solid wood, until they rested on the coverlet. Then the angel sat on the footboard and smiled at him with such compassion that the President felt a sob catch in his throat. Its eyes were filled with love. He wanted to weep. He passed one hand across his eyes, in hopes the hallucination would disappear, but when he opened them again, it was still there, resting its elbow on one knee and contemplating him, head cocked with puzzlement.

The President spoke aloud. "Aren't you going to tell me to Fear Not?"

He meant it as a joke, the quick good humor that had won him six elections before a landslide presidential race. It came out too loud and his voice quavered at the end. The angel, startled, faded almost into dusk. At the same moment, the President heard a knock on the door.

"Are you all right, sir?" It was Frank, his aide-de-camp, his valet, his guardian and guard. The angel shimmered dimly on the bed.

"I'm fine," he said. "Go to sleep. I'm just talking to myself."

He sat up higher in bed and tucked a pillow behind his back. The silence drew out and the angel reappeared full force, an aurora of colors flaming in the room. He caught his breath, for the light was blinding him and the colors were no longer in front of his eyes but inside them too, and the light was no longer at the foot of the bed but surrounding him. He was electrified with heat. Again he cried aloud. Frank opened the door.

"Sir? Do you need anything?"

Officious bastard, thought the President. He lay on the pillows, washed in light. All he wanted was to be left alone.

"Your light's burned out," said Frank, and he slammed his kneecap against the bed. "It's black as pitch in here. I'll get a bulb." He knew the President didn't like the dark.

The President wondered why he bothered when the room was full of light. He wondered why Frank did not comment on the angel smiling from the foot of the bed. His next thought was whether he was having a stroke or possibly dreaming. But Frank screwed the new light bulb into the lamp and turned on the switch.

"There." He shook the old bulb at his ear, then looked puzzled. "Oh. It wasn't dead." He tossed it in the trash basket anyway, not having registered his own words. "Good night, sir. Sleep well."

"Good night, Frank," the President said, and relaxed into that radiating light, the angel flaring, flaming on his bed.

The Premier sat bolt upright in bed. The angel stood, colossal and rectilinear. It was so large that its head touched the ceiling, brushing against the decorative plasterwork. In one hand it held a sword, hilt up, and from every corner of the room he could hear singing, a paean of praise.

The Premier, who had grown up in the godless state and never set foot in a church, crossed himself. Slowly the light went out. Slowly the angel disappeared.

And no one knew anything untoward had happened in the Enemy capital. The Premier did not mention it. He was ashamed of his gesture—a superstitious cross. Several times during the next days, he tried to erase it. He didn't know how. In his imagination he traced a backward cross. And once, in defiant rage, he tried the Star of David over the soiled spot. Heart, throat, forehead: How did his hand know exactly how to make a cross? For a week after the apparition, he found it hard to sleep. His mouth turned down in a grimace and his aides slunk by or jumped to do his bidding. The Premier's mood was black. Little things set him off. He made ferocious decisions. He took a mistress. He was not about to allow an apparition to deflect him from his appointed course.

* * *

The morning after the angel appeared, the President found himself thinking about the apparition during a meeting with the Joint Chiefs of Staff, and again in the afternoon with his economic advisors. He caught himself up short. He had too much to do to day-dream about the implications of a spirit realm. Later in the week he asked Rosemary, his secretary, to call his doctor: He had the beginnings of a cold, he said, but don't tell anyone the doctor had been called. The last thing he wanted was the Press on his tail.

"Have you ever known anyone who had apparitions, John?"

"Only madmen." The doctor laughed. "Why? You seeing things now?" John Deering had been the President's physician for twenty years.

"Not likely. Book I was reading last week. Can't even remember the name of it now," the President lied. "But the question was raised about whether everyone seeing things is sick. The author's premise was, no."

"It makes for dramatic impact, I suppose. Breathe out."

The stethoscope lay cold against his skin.

"Your lungs are clear. Stress would make you see things. What kind of apparitions?"

"Oh." The President gave a hearty laugh: "Ghosts, spirits, angelic manifestations. Whatever."

"Overwork would do it," the doctor said, pulling

his ophthalmoscope out of its case. "Did the character in the book actually see them wide-awake or just dream them in his sleep?"

"Saw them, wide-awake. Waking up from sleep. In the book they turned out to be real," the President added.

"Well, they never are. Hold still. If I were seeing things or dreaming them, I'd attribute it to stress, or maybe food intolerance or lack of exercise. You're fit as a fiddle, Matt. Do you get enough sleep?"

"Oh sure. They keep guard on me."

"Wake up in the middle of the night?"

"I read for a while."

"Have trouble going back to sleep?"

"Sometimes."

"Trouble eating? Loss of appetite?"

"No."

"Feeling low? Depressed?"

"They work me here." He realized he had lied for the last two questions.

In the end the doctor prescribed a mild sleeping pill and cautioned his friend to get more exercise, an hour a day if possible. He recommended swimming, but anything the President liked would do.

That night the President took two pills. The angel did not come. The next morning he climbed through drugged and heavy clouds to reach the light of day.

In those days, the major problem confronting the two Empires was economic. The U.S. subsisted as a garrison state, as did its sister nation, the Eastern Orthodox. Arms and armaments comprised the major sale commodity of both nations. These were sold to the lesser nations in the world, which resold them to each other. Food was scarce, but arms of war remained the major standard of 'currency. Arms had the advantage of always going out of date. Also they were expensive. They required hard machinery and high technology, an educated populace to service them, and constant replenishment of parts.

They served small purpose beyond the scope of war, which is to say, the destruction of one's enemies. This kept the focus of attention of every nation turned on the enemies whom the weapons were supposed to guard against.

Since weapons were the major currency of the world, the only way to pay for them was through interest-bearing loans from the banks of the civilized, armament-producing nations. Sometimes one or another small country would default on a loan, or not pay interest on its debt, as happened with several Latin countries. It created economic panic. Then the banking nations, which were located north of the Equator, met in convocation and decided by a mental and mathematical prestidigitation to rearrange the terms. Feeling much better, they so advised the nations to the south. The entire system was a house of cards held together by the willing suspension of disbelief.

"But that can't stick," said the President, when the

situation was first explained. His economic advisors assured him that it could, for the nation was enjoying unprecedented growth, due to the sales of armaments.

"The only thing holding the framework together, then, is the agreement of the banks and loaning nations to hold it together, is that right?"

"Yes sir," answered the head of the Federal Reserve.

"It's an illusion," the President said.

"It's not an illusion if we all agree it's real."

The President thought of the story of the Emperor parading naked down the street.

"All that's needed," he told the head of the Federal Reserve, "is one little child to shout, 'He hasn't any clothes!' The whole structure will come tumbling down around our ears."

"You forget the rest of the story, Mr. President." The chairman of the Chase Manhattan Bank leaned forward, grinning wickedly. The ice cubes tinkled in his scotch.

"Oh?" said the President. "What's that?"

"The little boy shouted: 'But he's naked. The Emperor has no clothes.' At which suddenly everyone could see the truth. The people were so shocked they turned on the child, and beat his brains out with cobblestones."

"Goodness." The President gave a laugh. The banker sank back in his chair and sipped his scotch.

The two White House economic advisors looked at him quizzically.

The banker nodded for emphasis: "Then the horses pranced, the flags waved, and the Emperor continued to sashay down the street. Everyone agreed he looked magnificent in his magic clothes."

At night sometimes the President thought of that. The economic recovery was based on fraudulent statistics. Rooms were filled with the calculations of computers. Forests fell for the paper on which to print the numerals that described the past or foretold the future growth of world economies.

The President knew the fiction could not be continued forever. At some point the economists would turn the page and find themselves at the end of the book.

The President was also concerned about the arms race. Nation after nation had nuclear weapons now: many of them overpopulated, and poor. Any one of them could detonate a weapon that would destroy a million or two of the ten billion people on the earth, leave a hole in the ozone layer, burn out the radiation shield that protected the eyes of mankind from the sun—as well as those of insects, dogs, and the pigeons in the air.

There were fifty thousand nuclear weapons in the mid-eighties. By the time of the events recounted here, these had increased to the hundreds of thousands in landscapes plotted and pieced—fold, fallow. . . . Everyone agreed they did not want nuclear war, but no one agreed on how to prevent it.

In the night, alone, the President lay awake. He was not sure if he was the Emperor or the child.

The President's name was Matthew. He was called Matt. His middle name was Madison, and his last name was Adams. He had won the election partly on his name. The name Adams recalled a period of principled Puritans. The name Madison recalled uneventful serenity, coupled with Virginia aristocracy. Matthew was the name of a saint, and Matt a comic book hero. His election occurred at a time when the nation felt nostalgic for high ideals. Very few people knew the President's forebears had taken the surname after dropping a Middle Eastern one. The country had been whiplashed by a decade of change. All it wanted was to stop.

Matt had the requisite presidential thick hair which he could run one hand through when he was putting on an "aw gee" act with the Press, and which, coupled with an engaging grin, could make a woman's heart twist. Also he was smart. He was direct, directed, and tough, and he had politically cunning advisors.

His concern was to run the country.

Theirs was to see that he got reelected at the completion of his term. The goals were sometimes contradictory, but until the President saw the angel at the foot of his bed, that did not bother him unduly. He was popular in the polls. Playing the part of a President may have been more important than being the President, he found. He had been astonished in his early days to discover . . . how little power he had. But he had the style that went with the perks that the people associated with power; and that was a form of power in itself. He could order a cup of coffee or a limousine. He could change his busy schedule at will, and pick up the telephone and call anyone in the world. He never had to handle money or pay a bill. He could walk into the War Room and spot (with a flick of an electronic switch) where every friendly submarine in the world lay hidden at that moment, and some of the enemy ones as well. He could spy on the missiles of the Eastern Empire. He could light boards with darting slashes to represent military units, his own or those of the Barbarians he played against. And he enjoyed it. But power is an elusive thing. It was diffused between a hundred units and a hundred thousand men and women, and at times it seemed to him that his job was merely to maintain the fiction of a monarch in command, while his advisors scurried like squirrels from one group to another, offering flattery, warnings, or rewards.

During the day, the President was kept too busy to wonder about the questions that pursued his nighttime dreams.

During the night he could not keep the dreams at bay.

Here is a dream he had after he saw the angel. He

was walking across a lawn of fallen leaves. The leaves were wet and mildewed from a long period of rain or perhaps from wet and mildewed skies. At the end of the lawn was a shallow pond. Its water was black. In it he could see the sodden leaves that had dropped to the muddy bottom. There was also a kind of sea grass that thrust like spiky eels above the surface. It was in every way unpleasant. He thought: I have to do this fast, or else I'll never dare. So he jumped in.

When he jumped, he realized he was wearing his favorite cashmere sweater and gray flannel pants, and the water was above his head. It was so cold he could not move, and he would drown if he did not begin to swim, but he could not move. He called for help. A woman, walking across the lawn, asked indifferently if he wanted cheddar or Jarlsberg cheese. . . .

He woke up trembling, struck by the joy of being still alive. Then he groaned at what the dream might mean. He took dreams seriously. Was it a warning that he was leaping without looking?

And if so, into what?

2

For many weeks that fall the angel did not reappear. The President had time to relax into himself. Also to take his soul by the scruff of the neck and scold it for deceiving him. In other words, he got a grip on himself. His staff relaxed as well under the beam of his easy smile. The President began to laugh at the apparition he had seen.

He even spoke of it to Frank. The valet, his white-haired, balding confidant, listened with his usual calm detachment. He neither ridiculed the idea nor accepted it.

"Crazy?" prompted Matt.

"I've seen too many impossible things," said the older man, "not to believe in impossibility."

"Nonsense!" snorted the President, annoyed to discover the responsibility for denouncing it lay fully on himself.

"You prefer a stroke?" Frank teased him gently.

The President laughed appreciatively. "Can't be that, because I'm fit and fine." He flexed his healthy biceps. "It was just a dream."

Then one night he sat up in bed with a gasp. The angel lit the room. It was garbed in gold, and the ceiling vanished in its burnished hair. The President's mouth went dry. Why didn't it speak? Its eyes burned into his soul, and what he felt was fear at its awesome majesty. He reached for a weapon—the brandy glass beside his bed—and threw it at the phantom with all his strength. The Waterford crystal skimmed through the figure of light to smash in splinters against the opposite wall.

"Demon," he breathed. "Who are you? What do you want with me?" His heart was running like footsteps in his chest.

The angel collected its aura into a firmer, smaller, more human shape. It shook itself, and ripples of light fell from its wings as it sent out a wave of love, of hope. Then to the President's wonderment, he saw the shattered glass begin to rise, re-form, rebuild, and the crystal was floating through the air, its drops of brandy at the bottom, to land softly on the table again.

At that moment the angel approached, until it

towered gorgeously above his bed, and now Matt saw that it was composed of stupendous colors, and down its flanks and, yes, off its wings, fell stars, cascading like liquid gold. It moved toward the President as if to enfold him.

"No!" he cried—but suddenly felt seized and then pulled forward, to plunge after the figure that swept through the bedroom door.

The halls were empty. The angel was a quivering, glorious presence ahead of him. He hurried on, down the red tongue of a rug, around a corner. He passed one sentry, sleeping, and wondered if this was all a dream.

The angel stopped at the north window. Again it gathered into human form, and again the President was stunned by a wave of such feeling that his knees went weak. He stepped back. He felt too dirty for such love.

It held up one hand—in caution? in blessing?—and flung itself through the closed glass pane.

The President ran forward. Had it disappeared? But no, he could see it shining in the night. It made him faint. Was this the same compassionate angel child that had first appeared to him, innocent as dawn? It crossed the lawn, melted through the metal bars of the spike fence, and floated across Pennsylvania Avenue, which was devoid of traffic at this hour.

In Lafayette Park across the street, the political protestors slept among their signs. MURDERER, one sign called silently, and ASSASSIN STOP WAR POLLU-

TION HOLOCAUST SAVE THE CHILDREN PRAY. The signs, intended to grab the President's attention, were as large as billboards. His reaction was disgust. Some of the others said:

SUE YOUR GOVERNMENT NOW
and
If Genocidal Weapons are Peacemakers,
ADOLF HITLER WAS A SAINT.

The park was populated by protesters, some of whom kept house in tents.

The angel turned, and the President knew it was directing his attention now to one ragged man, seated on a worn gray rug. He saw the angel flare with light. He saw him touch the beggar's shoulders, and felt a pang of jealousy, because now the beggar, too, was flaring, flashing luminescent. . . . The angel towered above the trees.

And then went out.

The President was left startled, staring, at black night. Across the street under the harsh glow of an incandescent street lamp, he could barely make out the beggar on his rug. He could see (but not read) the hideous signs about the President being a puppet of militarism, capitalism, and a fascist tool. . . .

The dry autumn leaves blew across the lawn in a little gust of wind.

* * *

In those days people were terrified of nuclear war. It had become a metaphor for the terror of their souls.

Since nuclear war posed a true and dazzling threat, no one remembered that for six millennia, or maybe ten, most of the people living on the planet had felt this anguish of existing, which comes from the grief at not; or that fear is the comrade of desire, or that their great desire was to fill the hole of sorrow around the heart. That's what they were trying to do. As soon as people named something of value, they found they were afraid of losing it. The more they valued it, and the more precious it appeared to them, the more they feared its loss, which would bring that sharp reminder of the void. Yet life is nothing but loss, beginning with the loss of the darkness at birth, when comfort explodes into pain, then the loss of childhood, the loss of innocence, the loss of friends, the loss of much-loved animals, of brothers, mother, father, the loss of investments, the loss of homes with their creaking floorboards and cribs and cozy nooks, the loss of jobs, the loss of dreams, and the repeated loss of self-esteem, and always hanging over them the loss that would be produced by their own death, the loss of the self that they would not even have gotten to know before it would be gone. Which is to say, the loss and extinction of the whole subjective world.

But here is the question: Why did the people in that generation elect to transfer their individual fear to the nuclear war? Or the Ring of Fire out in space?

There had always been war.

Indeed at the very time when the President saw the angel, no fewer than sixty-three wars were raging in one area or another. People didn't try to stop these wars, although they claimed to have a terrible concern for death. Or life, depending on how you look at it.

War had always been with them. War was fun. When the Moguls swept into India in the 1400s, they killed every man and male child and raped every woman they could find in order to spread their seed. They burned towns and villages. And then they built gardens and palaces, because no civilized people could live without gardens, they said.

To those who would eventually be killed, the devastation undoubtedly appeared as violent, ruthless, dramatic, and *final* (the light blinked out) as would any nuclear holocaust. No one in the area was left unaffected by the Mogul attack.

In all centuries wars raged like a contagion.

Why was the Ring of Fire different? Because it did not permit the dance to continue between human aspiration and despair, since people could no longer enjoy gambling at the game of Loss. It did not permit the terrible tension between the urge to create and the urge to destroy, or the paradox that from destruction springs the creativity of birth.

The winds of the Earth would whirl the radiation from even the smallest explosion right around the planet, and poison the mothers of the very people who set it off. Their skin would boil like milk; and if the eyes of bees would burn, what would happen to the eyes of their own little children, or of themselves?

The thing that scared the world was that the victors were threatened with destruction too, merely in order to play a little, to dice at the game of Loss.

Many people thought it took the fun out of killing.

3

The President knew he was going mad.

The morning after he saw the angel wrapped as a ball of fire, he called Jim Sierra, of Domestic Affairs, to the Oval Office.

"Who the hell is that beggar in Lafayette Park?" The words hit with no introduction, as Jim, thin, wiry, stepped in the door.

"Sir?" he asked.

"There's a tramp in Lafayette Park."

Jim gave a laugh. "There're a lot of tramps in Lafayette Park. Give me a clue which one."

The President smiled his famous grin. He appreciated Jim's humor and didn't want to make things worse. Right: nice and easy now, or surely Jim would diagnose him as insane.

"You know that bunch of demonstrators across from the White House? There's a whole camp of them there, with their ugly signs, their tents. Some are living on the sidewalk. One of them sits cross-legged on a gray blanket, staring at the White House door."

"Yes?"

"I don't give a damn how you do it, but get them out of there. I don't want to see them again."

"All of them?" Jim's shock registered on his face. He thought of the demonstrators, twenty, forty, maybe fifty of them at any given time; they came and went; they took a turn of so many hours or so many weeks and were replaced by other Believers from other states. They were organized. They sat, stood, slept, spoke soapbox speeches in Lafayette Park, marched to other cities as a protest, waved flags and banners, and camped on the grass.

"They're protected by the Constitution," he said thoughtfully. His first loyalty was to the presidency. His second was to the pleasure of solving problems efficiently, with mathematical purity. "We can't just clear them out by the police. The Press would get on it. You'd have a hundred more demonstrators tomorrow, and five hundred after that, if you kept carting them off. They're permitted to sit there."

"I don't care how you do it." The President was ashamed to say his interest lay in one man only, one filthy vagrant who might not even belong to the demonstrators, who sat on a gray blanket on the cement sidewalk—sleeping on the heating grates, perhaps—who knows what he did when it got cold?

"Get an ordinance," he said. "Get the courts to say they can't demonstrate so close to the White House."

"They used to sit right in front of the White House, on the sidewalk there," Jim said, shooting the cuffs of his immaculate tailored suit. "They were moved across the street to Lafayette Park." The homeless. The wanderers. The ill. The nomads. All of them eyesores in an unsightly world. No way to care for them in a depressed economy.

They had been moved out once before in the 1980s, only to return after a victorious ACLU suit.

"Then they can be moved again. Or pick them up for loitering and take them to a shelter. Clothe them. Feed them. Lock 'em in jail. Just get them the hell out of my sight."

He turned back to the papers on his desk.

In those times, weapons had names. Like gladiators. Some of the names were fashioned from letters and numerals: ABM, MX, SSN-21.

Another group of weapons had names of charming innocence: Cruise missiles. They sounded like friendly postcards from romantic ports of call. Some had affectionate nicknames or diminutives, like Midgetman. Or Daisy Wheel. And some had names to strike terror in the hearts of man: Sleuth, Stealth, Strike, Storm.

Mostly the harsh glottals were preferred by the military poets. (It is a mistake to presume the two words form an oxymoron: military/poet. Simply that they hear a different drum.) The poets who named the gladiator weapons wore stars on their uniforms and gold braid on their hats. Their mouths, like those of fish, were composed of a single curving line, downturned.

Their business was destruction. They took it seriously.

In those days the poets were also playing with intergalactic laser-beam weapons. It was the Ring of Fire, pure mathematics, which is synonymous with poetry. A balance. Purity. Like a fine golf shot.

In their efforts to make the opposition aware of the perfect beauty of the perfect mathematical golf shot, in an effort to express their thoughts more clearly, they repeated their same arguments louder. Their opponents were also poets, who saw not the perfect balanced shot, landing a hole-in-one in space, but a fatal accident in which the club itself falls back to earth and probably incinerates the whole course, including the city they themselves lived in, their house and dog, and also their own children, their immortality. Given the perfect inconsistency of chance and accidents (itself a kind of mathematical poetry), they preferred safer games than intergalactic golf.

The military poets did not understand why the antistellar pacifists did not hear peace, as they did, when words of war were sung. The pacifists did not understand why songs of war were heard when they preached peace.

At one time the warriors would appear to win, and then trillions and quadzillions would be appropriated for development of weapons that could ride on solar winds; at another time the opposition would be in precedence, and all work on the systems would stop. For years it had gone on that way.

The reason that both sides kept repeating the same arguments, increasing only the decibels, is that neither could believe that its opponents could listen and yet disagree. Therefore they spoke louder. Or at a higher pitch. Thinking they hadn't been heard.

What they were squabbling about was the best way to have peace.

4

After he saw the angel, the President found he knew things. He first noticed it at a staff meeting. He looked over at General Wallace across the board-room table and saw he was thinking of his gambling debts; and also whether his wife had taken his uniform to the cleaners; he was being taken to the cleaners, and he was goddamned if he would let the enemy clean-sweep our country, his country, his beautiful clean country, making promises they wouldn't keep. You couldn't trust the dirty Empire.

He looked at Admiral Epps, a fine, ruddy-faced man with a broad grin and an easy way of spreading his freckled hands, palms down on the table before him; a likable man, with a sparkle in his eyes and a ready laugh. The President saw him breaking eggs in an iron skillet, the yolks and whites running—

"You look fit." He leaned over to Admiral Epps, whispering behind his hand. "What did you have for breakfast this morning?"

"Fried eggs," Epps whispered back. "But not as good as when I cooked them myself. Mess servants," he finished with a cheerful grimace. Nonetheless, the yolks spread in his stomach in an aura of well-being.

At this staff meeting, Jim Sierra (Domestic Affairs) fought as usual with Steven Dirk (Internal Affairs)—the two men always disagreed.

Jim leapt nervously to his feet, then sat again and shot his cuffs: "For Christ's sake, Steve. That's the worst idea you've come up with yet. Run to Congress with that baby and they'll slaughter us."

The President intervened. "Why?" he asked quietly.

"Look, Kelly's for it." Jim counted off his fingers angrily. "Tim, Mark Hatter . . . In all I count fucking thirty-two. That's all. Wallace and Andrews are both waffling—waiting to catch the wind. And if you can't get them, you've got fucking shit. We'll come away eating fucking shit."

That's how men in power talked. Matt had not noticed it before.

"But we have Tony and Governor Butts," argued the President, coming in on Steve Dirk's side. "The liberals. We can call in debts."

"Don't bet your ass." Jim's mouth turned down.

"Those bastards'll chuck you to the crocodiles. They haven't a fucking shred of integrity, and Chung Wu isn't what we ..."

But the President wasn't listening, because with surprise he saw Jim's jaw still open, gaping, talking, and then he saw only the maw of the mouth and yellowed teeth. Jim's anger flared in horns from his hair; his dark eyes burned. And it was not his angry words Matt heard, but hate. And below the hate another layer, so that Matt covered his eyes with one hand, because the layers were peeling away with terrifying speed: below the anger, hate; below the hatred, fear. Fear hovered before the President's wide view. *It's yellow*, he thought simplistically; and watched in fascination the discovery that the metaphor for cowardice is factual reality. The color yellow played around Jim's head. It lay inside his voice. He was like a pitcher pouring yellow silence on the mahogany table, and it spread into puddles before the council members and Joint Chiefs of Staff.

In a moment the vision was gone. The President could breathe again.

"Is something wrong?" Stan asked.

The President removed his glasses and pressed two fingers in the corners of his eyes. "I'm listening," he said. "Jim, write me a memo, with your views, and, Steve, you do the same. One page."

The President dismissed the meeting, grateful that no one guessed what he had seen. At the doorway, he placed one hand on Jim's shoulder in a familiar way.

"Are you all right?" the President asked when the others were out of earshot. "Things okay with Susan and you?"

"Fuck it." Jim laughed. "How do you know that? We had a fight last night. She's asking for a divorce."

The President nodded, wondering why he thought Jim had thrown a plate of fish against the wall.

"I threw a plate of fish in the kitchen," Jim said. He shook his head sheepishly. "Damn stupid thing to do, but Jesus I was mad."

"You can get back together," said the President.

"I don't *want* her," said Jim. "Let her come on her hands and knees, I wouldn't fucking take her back."

"Come inside."

When the door closed on them, he threw himself in a chair and rocked back, feet on the desk. "Anything I can do?"

"No sir. She says I work too hard. Hell, what does she expect? She knew that when she married me. She thinks the White House shuts down at night? Sure, I'm tense. So what else is new. And her going off with some guy behind my back. She's got a *friend*, she says."

"A lover?" the President asked abstractly.

"Who the hell knows. He listens to fucking classical music, if you can imagine. That's what she likes." And Jim gave a hoarse grunt that was meant to pass for a laugh. "Anyway, I don't talk to her about my work. No need for worry there, sir."

The President nodded. "If you don't talk about work, you must have little to say."

"That's what she says. Actually we don't have a helluva lot to talk about. The kids. Hell, we've been married thirteen years, what does she expect?"

The President could not answer. Had his marriage with Anne been any better? "What do you expect?" he asked.

"I'll tell you what I expect," Jim answered vehemently. "I expect a person to stand by their word. She made a vow at the altar of God. I don't believe in God, but you make a promise, you goddamn well stick by it."

"And if you don't?"

"And if you don't, where are any of us, anyway? That's all we've got, isn't it? The law. Our promises. You should be punished, that's all."

"Politics breeds bad marriages." The President came to his feet. He wanted to say much more. You'll live through it. This is an opportunity, if you take the dare. Or perhaps he wanted to say that all marriages go through bad times. Hang in there. There were things he could tell about himself and Anne, and private pains he knew. Or maybe he wanted to tell Jim to go home now, take off the afternoon and spend some time with his wife, as he had not done years ago when the business first came up with Anne.

Instead he said nothing. Jim's face closed over his pain.

At the door the President said: "Get me that memo soon as you can."

He put in a full day's work. He read what had to be read, was briefed on the latest emergencies, signed papers, authorized others for his automatic signature. He posed for photographers, smiling triumphantly over a ceremonial award. He visited an honorary grave and had tea with a visiting minister of state, which became, at his insistence, a scotch and soda. And he smiled and waved for the camera's eye.

In other words, he behaved as people liked their President to do. His special mark as President was simple: He made it look like fun.

But at night, the state dinner over, and he again in his room, where Frank was laying out his pajamas and taking away his clothes to wash and press, the two of them moving quietly around one another, he began to chew his pain.

All day he had known the inner thoughts of those about him—the uneasiness of the foreign minister of state, and how he was playing France against the USA. Sometimes he saw the knowledge as a cloud around a man, and other times he simply knew that something was wrong: A lie was being told, though he might not know the nature of the lie. He saw pain without knowing its source. And cobwebs of loneliness. And an aureole of rage. And also fear. As if he'd lost three layers of skin.

He climbed into bed and lay against the pillows. He didn't know what troubled him the most: the state of his advisors or himself. How could he trust the political judgment of a man so angry he would throw a plate at the red-painted kitchen wall? (White flakes of fish oozing down the red wall and behind the radiator.) Jim's wife had gasped in shocked surprise. Jim had almost hit her instead, and the President saw that too, as clearly as if he had been in the room. He considered General Wallace as well, pressed by personal debts, projecting, under his aggression, fear. . . . Was everyone acting, and calling on him to act, in response to personal fears?

On the other hand he himself, Matt Adams, was maybe going mad. He turned that over in his mind. He was afraid of that.

"Good night, Mr. President," said Frank at the door, jacket and trousers over one arm, the President's shoes dangling from his fingertips.

"Good night, Frank."

"Are you all right, sir?"

It was the second time that day one of his staff had asked.

"I'm fine. Do I look sick?"

"Just that you seem distracted."

"Ah. Well, good night, Frank."

He returned to his train of thought. He felt in perfect condition. His skin looked tanned, his body fit. He exercised, drank in moderation, did not smoke. How, then, to explain these flashes of imagination? Were they due to a short circuit on the pathways of the brain? Incipient stroke?

Whatever was happening, he could not speak of it. Neither could he enter a hospital for tests. No one knew better than the President the dangers of letting the opposition entertain the slightest doubt. There was no one he could talk to. He stood alone.

Frank was not the only member of the White House staff to be concerned about the President. Every eye was fixed on him, for the moods of the monarch affect everyone.

In the basement cafeteria, secretaries dropped coins into machines to release a cold, dank sandwich wrapped in plastic, or an apple that had been kept eight months in cold storage, or a white paper cup into which a brownish liquid flowed. It was called tea or coffee or bouillon, but tasted much the same in any case.

As they stood at the machines, purchasing their lunch, they complained in cautious undertones about their bosses, or more loudly about the weather, or their boyfriends, or, in a more general way, of the day. They cast their moods onto the rain or allergies or the barometric pressure of the memos going out that day, or on their hangovers from the night before, which was probably the only truthful one in the list. Nerves were on edge these days. Everything was being done at top speed, with overtime, and little sleep, and the sense of frenzy and hurry was infectious. In the Eastern Orthodox it was said that the

Premier's hands shook. Rumor circulated he had Parkinson's disease. The White House waited, pondering the meaning of that turn of events, and who was governing. Intelligence (capital I) reported a wave of repression throughout that Empire, the crackdown being strongest on the news. Therefore no one knew what was going on. Rumors spread also of a military buildup or preparation for invasion.

The secretaries felt the undercurrent of electricity in the Presidential Palace. It gave them pleasant shudders of excitement, for they knew the importance of their work. They hurried back upstairs, to eat their wet cardboard sandwiches at their desks.

In the staff dining room, Jim Sierra sat at a table spread with a linen cloth. Linen napkins were folded into fans in each water tumbler, and the silverware gleamed. He ate with Norman Schwartzjenna, the Chief of Staff, with Steve Dirk, Internal Affairs, and with Bill Garcia, External Affairs. The conversation always revolved around politics and the President.

Not long before, at a state dinner, the President had sat in brooding silence. He had twirled his wineglass and glowered under his brows at the assembly, too absorbed to talk to the white-haired wife of a mining magnate on his left, or to the dyed-blond wife of the prime minister of a large European country on his right. Fifty sophisticated people, the First Lady at their head, had therefore carried the conversation by themselves. Which they did, and well enough, though the President's silence cast a pall. He was not his usual light, laughing, wicked, witty self.

Then, at dessert, the President had suddenly turned to the visiting dignitary from India, seated beyond one of his own dinner partners, caught his eye, and interrupted:

"Do you believe in God?"

"Oh yes." The Ambassador had nodded amiably. "God, yes. Everyone wise worships a deity."

Official Washington thought the Ambassador a fool. He spoke in a lilting English that placed the rhythms on all the wrong words. He smiled at the slightest notice, the grin opening his dark face.

"They don't worship the same one, though," the President shot back. "And no one can agree on how God works. Is it a beneficial force or—"

"Yes, beneficial, very good."

"—a punishing, threatening God?"

"Yes, punishing too. Very hard." He nodded, always smiling. It was such inconsistencies that made the President view him with contempt.

"Sometimes he is playful too, do you not think?" the Ambassador continued. "We have a view of God as a little child playing in a garden with his toys. Do you like that? He is very playful, God."

"And what do you believe in, Mr. President?" asked Emily Stanhill, the wife of the mining magnate.

He turned from the Indian Ambassador and stared at her without answer, and at that moment another guest leaned forward curiously: "What's the question?"

The President recovered himself. "The question is: Is there a divine intervention in the affairs of man? In fact, is there anything at all, divine or not? Is there a God?"

"Oh, of course there is."

"Then second, is He looking out for us?" cried another at the table. "That's the question! What's God's responsibility to Man?" He sat back triumphantly, challenging his dinner partners, either side.

"And after that," said the mining magnate's wife, "what is our responsibility to God? Do you pray, Mr. President?"

The President shot her a startled look, but before he could respond, the butler was at his arm. It was time to rise for coffee in the East Room and hear a chamber orchestra.

"No," he said, offering her his arm. "Do you think I should?"

In the East Room they sat on uncomfortable, small, gilded chairs with red velvet seats. The President, seated beside the First Lady, was observed to be lost again in thought. At the conclusion of the first piece, he rose, bowed gravely to his wife and guests, and left.

The next morning the public relations office went bananas with phone calls. The staff didn't know which was of more concern: that the President had walked out on his duties, or that he had engaged in that extraordinary table conversation, which would not have mattered except it was somehow reported in the Press.

"What do you think is going on?" Jim asked the group at his luncheon table.

"Something's wrong," said Steve.

"He's isolating. I wasn't even sure he was present at the meeting this morning."

"It's as if he's listening to something else."

"He asked for a Bible," Jim blurted out, ashamed of his report.

"Good God!" It was accompanied by an embarrassed laugh.

"Did you get him one?" asked Norman, the Chief of Staff.

"I got him a Bible and a Hindu Bhagava-whatsis, to remind him it's only a book."

"Look, he can read the Bible," said Steve, Internal Affairs. "Nothing wrong with that. A Bible by his bedside, why the hell shouldn't he? Make sure the Press learns of it. Drop it casually. The President always reads the Bible at night. Great publicity."

Bill Garcia, External Affairs, added: "I think we ought to do more with religion anyway. He ought to go to church occasionally."

"Different ones," said Jim. "Jewish, Catholic, Protestant."

"Sure, hell, invite a bishop or a cardinal to the White House. It couldn't hurt."

"Jesus, who the hell would we get?"

That's the way they talked, these ministers of state.

5

The angel stayed away.

Those nights when the President awoke, he roamed the carpeted corridors of his palatial prison, past sleeping guards.

He stood a long time at one tall window. The floodlights gave a perfect view of lawns. He padded to his private kitchen to raid the little fridge that was stocked with ice cream and delicacies for just such nocturnal fits. He wanted to be held. He remembered how he once could slip into his wife's bed and snuggle with her in the years before— "Before," he called it to himself, with a capital B. But he had no desire these days for her, and often not for any other woman, though of course he sometimes feigned lust

still, in order to be one of the Boys. He was known
to love women, and certainly women loved him. If
he slept alone, it was by choice.

He waked the dozing sentries with his restless
steps.

"Mr. President?" they murmured. "Sir?"

He waved them back to sleep. "No problems. I'm
all right."

Nights passed. Days. He knew he lied, that things
were anything but well. Great sighs broke from his
lips. He did not know the source of his unease.

He wanted help. You will ask why he did not
speak to someone, find a kindred heart, seek out a
doctor or psychiatrist who might heal the heart or
mind—or, lacking that, a spiritual director or guide,
a minister to the soul. But to whom could he go? In-
fected minds to their deaf pillows will discharge their
secrets; and what he needed, he did not know. In
that time tradition dictated that the President would
not practice religion, although political speeches
were laced with godly references, precedent dying
hard. Neither was it considered appropriate for a
President to be in need of a doctor to the mind, a
psychiatrist. In fact, the very opposite. If he required
that kind of help (it was argued), then he must be
unfit to lead the country. It is a hard custom that
says you grind away your soul rather than ask for
help.

The official and proclaimed reason no President
went to church (none having done so for years) was

fear of assassination. An assassination attempt (it was explained) would unfairly disrupt church services for the other worshipers. No one questioned the argument. Fear was the predominant emotion of that age. Any action could be justified on the grounds of fear and found perfectly acceptable as rational or cautionary; and those in the Intelligentsia, who prided themselves on having displaced superstition with Science, emotion with Reason, did not make the connection that any fear, including their own, was merely an emotion too, like hope.

Hope, and also much that led to hope, was usually said to be "unrealistic." Which is why religion and its improbable, unproved optimism were frowned upon. In that age "being realistic" was a synonym for "pessimistic," so fashionable was despair.

And the angel stayed away.

The park bums were gone. The earth turned on its axis, unaware, and the sun rose and fell, morning and evening, in gorgeous, splashy colors like banners, saying Look at Me! Only God could create so vulgar a display and get away with it.

And Matt's heart burned—with an emptiness so profound that tears sprang into his eyes if he allowed himself even to approach with one sensitive tentacle his inner being: the void! Oh Christ! The hollow at his heart. He had not even noticed it until that night the angel appeared.

Now he talked to himself, or was it to this missing entity he had seen?

"I'm so angry," he said. "I'm so hurt. Alone. Oh God! I'm alone!"

That's how he prayed in those days of desolation, in the winter of his discontent, when he didn't even know that these were prayers or pleas for help, but only conversations with his empty heart.

One night the President's entourage swept through the wet, slick streets of the nighttime city, past the glinting lights of empty offices, roads cleared of other cars. He leaned back against the cushions beside Anne, his wife, whose plump right hand rested lightly on the window, the other in her lap, and who stared unseeing out her window, miles away. Her brown hair was pulled back on her neck with a pearl and diamond clasp. She sat too straight, the lonely, angry queen.

The entourage consisted first of a police car, siren screaming, roof lights whirling red and white. This was followed by four motorcyclists, riding two by two, and then a bulletproof car of secret service bodyguards, guns at the ready. The President's black limousine came next, its occupants hidden behind smoked glass. Flags fluttered on the front fenders. It dragged in its wake, like a comet's tail, more secret service cars, a dummy limousine, an open jeep with mounted machine gun, and a final octad of mounted motorcycle cops.

They were approaching the White House gates when the accident occurred. One forward motorcyclist, braking, slithered on the slippery street and lost control. He jumped a curb, righted, then twisted around in his efforts to maintain control and, one tire blown (bang!), skidded under the wheels of the approaching secret service van. The police fanned out in case he had been the victim of a sniper's gun—the explosion of a tire: bang! Their man lay bleeding under the van. They rushed to positions, guns ready, in their haste to protect the President.

Accidents create accidents.

The chauffeur gunned his limousine—and stalled. Frantically he turned the ignition, listening to the dry churn of the motor. A dozen men surrounded the limousine, guns drawn.

In the back seat Matt's eyes fell on the figure lit by the streetlight in Lafayette Park. He sat wet and in rags on a gray blanket on the sidewalk. Above his head was a woman's purple silk umbrella. It did not keep off the rain. Beside him was a sign: PEACE NOW. ANGER, VIOLENCE BREED SAME.

Their eyes met, and an electric charge ran through the President—of what? Revulsion? Hate? The anticipated pleasure of a fight? He pulled his eyes away and banged on the glass that separated him from his chauffeur.

"Get this car moving!" he shouted angrily.

"Matthew, please," Anne murmured beside him.

At that moment it caught and lurched ahead, snapping him back against the seat. Another moment and the limousine had turned into the White House drive. The gates clanged shut. He was safe.

But as he strode into the White House, the President was furious. He himself did not know why. He grabbed the first secret service agent that he passed.

"Why the hell is that vagrant back in Lafayette Park?" Rage consumed him.

"Sir?" The agent was startled.

"Under the purple umbrella. I told you to get him out of there."

And he took the stairs two at a time, without waiting for an elevator.

That night, the President stalked the corridors of the upstairs rooms, pacing. He refused to take a sleeping pill. He wanted his mind clear, yet all he knew was turmoil and unwelcome restlessness.

At one point he stood at a window overlooking Pennsylvania Avenue. From there he could see across the green lawns, raked of November leaves. He looked through a lattice of the limbs of trees. Under the passionate white streetlights of the avenue, he could see the tramp, who sat, legs crossed yogi fashion, facing the White House. No purple umbrella covered him. His face was in shadow. Dharma bum.

The President turned away with a grimace and returned to his room.

He fell asleep like a stone dropping through water, and sometime later, a turtle swimming with powerful, slow strokes, he rose to the surface of his consciousness again, took one quavering, sighing breath and opened his eyes.

He remembered the question: How could they have exchanged a look at night through the protection of blackened glass? The windows of the limousine were smoked, to prevent observers from seeing inside. But those eyes had looked directly into his, the eyes of the man the angel had touched.

The President was filled with longings he could not understand. He was struck by the fragility and ferocity of life. What did the angel mean by bowing to a tramp? Then, lying in bed, he remembered something else. It is a cardinal rule of the physical universe that we cannot see through a solid. No one, holding a book, can see all sides at once. We have to turn it in our hands; or if the object is too big to hold, then walk around it to observe the other side.

But standing at the north window only hours earlier, when, after the accident, he had stared out at that disreputable shape, Matt had seen all sides of the vagrant at once. He had seen his cracked leather shoes, set neatly on the grass behind him. He had seen the newspaper pushed into the seat of his pants to keep out cold. He had seen his thin shirt under his worn jacket, and his bare ankles tucked under him. He had seen his fingernails caked with dirt, and yes, his unclipped toenails too.

Matt had not questioned how he could see such detail across a hundred and fifty yards. Only now, lying in his bed, eyes open in the darkness, did the questions come.

He remembered also that when the angel (he now

called it that) had disappeared and blackness took its place, the darkness had seemed more intense for the blinding quality of that earlier light. Yet there were streetlights on. Why would he have seen the night as dark? Night is never black in Washington, where lights burn all the time and reflect off the clouds with a dull orange glow. When she had disappeared (he now called it "she"), the President had felt his soul lunge out of his body to join her, and then snap back with pain. For souls can't easily leave their physical shells. Also he had felt the contradictory and delicious malice of her having left—gone from the indigent she honored. Gone from him, the President, gone from making him insane.

He lay awake a long time, thinking of these impossibilities.

6

Suddenly it was clear to the President that he had no control over anything.

Some of the problems beyond the President's hands were:

Famine in the sub-Sahara, fostering exiles and war.

The spread of deserts to the east.

The burning of forests in the southern hemisphere.

Wars on almost every continent of the globe.

Drought in the Midwest grain fields.

Disease in the cattle of the West.

Flood in the Southwest deserts. The water stood

eight feet deep in the streets of one dry town, while rivers to the north were drying up.

Meanwhile, restless nomads pushed across the frontiers from the south. The intrusion was illegal, but the hordes were poor and hungry, drawn by hope. They walked at night and melted into urban alleyways by day. The police could not find a fraction of them, and those they did remove simply turned around when once released and attempted the crossing again.

The President ruled an ungovernable nation. The military was growing in power, as the possibility of war increased. In a reluctant peacetime the officers had nothing to do but skulk in their offices, play golf, and plan for wars that often did not come; or else form petty factions, and dream of more belligerent times. But now, the blast of war blown in their ears, they were like tigers, pacing, ready. Throughout the world rode the four horsemen of fire, famine, disease, and death. With them trotted war, sniffing at the carrion of distress.

The President had won election on a platform of Four E's, or For Ease: Energy, Education, Equality, Economy. But any action seemed to provoke an opposing counterforce of harm elsewhere.

I won't describe specifics of the policies nagging his decisions every day. But one night the President had a thought about the Border Treaty, at the fringes of the war. He telephoned his aide at home.

"Is Jim there?"

It was one A.M. The pause lengthened. "Hello?" he repeated. "Is Jim Sierra there?"

"Jim doesn't live here." Her voice came at him taut, through clenched teeth. "He lives at the White House."

"This is the President calling." He had no time for games. "Can I speak to Jim?"

"Listen, it is one o'clock in the morning. I don't know who you are and I don't care. Jim Sierra hasn't lived here for weeks. He lives in the White House, with the other automatons. Or else he's with some chick. So don't come clamoring around real people— his wife and kids. If you're looking—"

"Is this Mrs. Sierra?" He was openly confused. "This is the President."

"Oh, sure," she answered, though she should have recognized his voice, and might have, had she been less upset or less certain it was a practical joke played on her by Jim. "And I'm the King of Siam. Why aren't you asleep like decent people, getting enough rest so you can do your job? Why aren't you letting your staff and advisors sleep? Give them time with their families? You think they make better decisions by never relaxing? You all run on adrenaline, you're hyped up, and then you think it's normal, what you do. In fact you think we owe you something for behaving like addicts, drugged on power. We owe you worship, right?"

"Mrs. Sierra—"

"You're drunk, aren't you? You get sotted and call the Old Lady in vengeance because she wants to kick out Jim. Well, you listen to me, buddy—"

For the first time Matt remembered Jim and Susan had split up. "Mrs. Sierra, I'm—"

"I'm better off without him. He's nearly psycho. You go tell that to the President. Jim's interested in one thing only."

"What's that?" She had Matt's full attention now.

"Power. He's hungry for power. And why? Well you may ask! Why indeed? To do good? Save mankind? No, but just to have a sense that maybe he exists. If you're the President, you understand that, don't you? Isn't that what you want too?"

"What? Explain it to me again?" How unlike him it was to hang on to the phone, tongue-tied. He could not take it from his ear.

"To feed your needy little ego. To delude yourself of your own importance. It's all a lie. You're little children playing in a sandbox with your toys. Who's got the biggest truck? That's the game. Where do you stand in the pecking order? This entire city's sick. The journalists think they don't exist unless they get a front page story once a week, and not only a byline, but above the centerfold. The Congress—for God's sake, those men don't even know the power they enjoy is the power of an office. They think it's *theirs*. The White House staff are sycophants, telling the President only what he wants to hear. You want to know how I know that too? Ha! I live with one. They ignore their children, their parents, their wives. Ask Jim how his mother is. When was the last time he went to visit the nursing home? Ask him what he's working for till all hours of the night, screwing the secretaries, I suppose. Ask him. I'd like to hear the reason why."

She stopped. The pause lengthened.

"Are you there?" she said.

"I'm listening."

"Then don't. Go away. Go to sleep. I have two children to raise. Go play with your trucks in the sandbox. Leave me alone, I don't care who you are."

"I profoundly apologize," he said. "I'm sorry to have woken you."

When she heard the phone click dead, she burst into tears. She cried uncontrollably, though she could not have told you why.

In the morning, the President had his secretary send a bouquet of camellias to Mrs. Sierra, with a handwritten apology on White House paper.

Matt wondered if Susan Sierra was right about Jim wanting power. He thought Jim wanted what all of humankind is longing for—acknowledgment. He wanted to be *seen*. He wanted someone to say, "I hear you; yes, I understand"—and thereby know that he was not alone.

It was not so difficult to comprehend. Matt guessed that Susan wanted the same thing. They both, probably, wanted the satisfaction of knowing that they, their work, would make a difference to the lives of others. True, Jim was rigid, controlling. True also that he worked to shut out a growing sense of futility. But why not?

When the President looked around him, he saw only men and women suffering. Was no one free of it? He looked at himself and he could see he had everything in the American dream. He was handsome, rich, competent, powerful. He walked in halls fit for princes and thousands at his bidding speed. He had hundreds of wonderful toys with which to play—boats and horses and airplanes and women and swimming pools, and pianos; houses in Vail and Martha's Vineyard, with food and furnishings in abundance. He had fishing rods, and ice skates and tennis rackets and rowing machines, weights and skis and billiard tables, whole libraries of books and a bowling alley; ranches in Montana, and computer rooms with all the information in the world. He could meet anybody he wished in the whole world. Yet what was any of it worth? Over him lay a cloak of desolation, which he thrust out of his consciousness as best he could—by play, by work. In work, especially at his level as monarch, he hoped to make his contribution, though usually he felt like an ancient king he'd read about as a boy, making proclamations to the tides.

Then the President, thinking of this despair and frustration, of his own futile efforts to make a difference to the world, wondered, for the very first time in his life, why? Why make a difference?

Lying in bed at night, he was struck by a thought he'd never bothered with before. Who am I? And why? Why bother with the betterment of humankind? He was ashamed, for this was the stuff of college kids' debates, not questions for grown men. To work for the betterment of anything implied belief in Progress (when in fact, he thought, there was no betterment, only constant change), and also it implied dissatisfaction with matters as they were. Was he so dissatisfied?

It took him many hours of consideration. This is what he decided. Humanity divides into two types. Some people want to make a difference to the lives of others. They work for Progress, or world harmony, or medical breakthroughs, or the rights of animals, or to create a masterpiece of art. Some few even consciously strive to heal or alleviate suffering or raise the consciousness of humankind.

Others—pirates, thieves, pickpockets, cutthroats, rapists, assassins, cheats, and con men—are out to help themselves.

Yet both types have a similar motive: to justify the fact that they are alive, the one by paying for the privilege somehow, the other by grabbing more of what they can.

The strategy differs, in other words, but the motives (he decided) are the same, for the former gain by giving, and the latter by taking. Yet Matt also imagined a third alternative. Could there be a person who works with no set goal, no particular outcome in his mind? This person would be neither giving nor grabbing, but rather *delighting* in or playing at what engages him, as if all thoughts and work and social intercourse were merely an adventure to be enjoyed. Matthew Adams, the President, didn't know anyone who lived like that, himself included, but it appeared to him to be a liberating attitude. Then all work would be play, without struggling to effect a particular result. You'd always win.

And it also occurred to him how utterly simple the answer to his question was: Who am I? What for? The answer was simply: Yes! For Joy!

The President understood all this with a clarity that astonished him. Life, the whole business, was a game, a dance. Susan was right. It was a bit of sandbox play. The only thing she hadn't understood is that that's the way it ought to be.

7

The President knew he was going crazy. He could no longer control his feelings, which swept through him like summer rainstorms—tears of horror or sorrow would be followed only hours later by delirious joy—or rapture, at the sight of . . . nothing! A vase of irises, for example, in the upstairs hall. He could have fallen to his knees in worship of the color blue, each petal licked by a gaudy yellow tongue. The spring flower had been flown in specially for the upstairs hall, and was exhibited against a stark white wall. He felt he had never seen before, as if his eyes had been veiled by cataracts, which, stripped away, left him dazzled by ordinary sights.

One day he saw a secretary walking up ahead and

stared as if he'd never seen the human form before. He was startled by his gratitude. Jim, seeing it, clucked his tongue in shared respectful lust, and the President, grown cunning in his madness, laughed and slapped his aide on the back and gave a rueful shake of the head. But his heart twisted in his chest like a dishrag, because what he had seen had everything and nothing to do with sex. Earlier that day, he had glanced out the window at an elm and been caught by the space between the branches, so that for a moment he felt the tree was he himself, and if he cut into the bark, he would hear it scream and see its blood, and his own arm would bleed in sympathy and his own tongue give cry. It was the same with the girl. She was Matt, he was her, though he had never tottered on high heels.

He jerked himself back to being President. "Not here," he muttered to his erection. He knew he was not well. He took to rubbing the bridge of his nose with thumb and forefinger, then sliding them out to the corners of his eyes to wipe away the tears.

Or he turned gruffly away from his aides and staff, lest they see how moved he was.

He wanted the angel to come back. He looked for it. He had questions to ask, but it did not reappear.

Sometimes he woke up in the mornings, his heart flooded with joy, and his body with a radiance so exquisite that he would lie in bed, eyes closed, quivering at the waves of light that pulsed through him. He was being made love to by waves of warmth and light. Then he turned to the window and saw the dawning of the new day, the cloud formations piling up beyond the trees, and felt his heart pulled out of his body by the rush of gratitude.

He wondered if anyone could see his rapture. Sometimes at work he pushed the papers aside, or cut the conversation short, unable to bear one more word of distrust, or to play "put-down," a game he had always enjoyed, though he'd called it "competition" then, or "playing to win." Why had he wanted to smash and shame the other fellow? To win a point? For what? To triumph over another, only to discover he was alienated from humanity.

He was too crafty to say all this out loud. He would push aside the papers and rise to his feet. "Gentlemen, we need more information. Write me a memo, Bob." (Or Jim, or John, or Jeffrey, or Jed.)

Neither could he bear the mystery novels any longer. He wanted something with more meat, though he could not have said what that meant. Or he wanted nothing to read at all. He wanted to dissolve into radiant light.

Here is another reason he knew things were awry: His feelings toward his wife began to change. He looked across the dining room table at this woman with whom he had lived for thirty-eight years, mother of his sons, and there was the fresh-faced college girl now hidden behind a matron's face, cheeks going heavy, and the skin of her eyelids wrinkling over her brown eyes.

When you live with a person for many years, you think you've learned their ways. You set them in a frame and see that portrait even though it may not represent that person anymore at all, but merely the image that she (or he) has become accustomed to holding up to you.

They had not shared their lives in years. Except in public. Political pretense, at which they both excelled. They held hands and smiled at each other's grins on camera and waved triumphantly from platforms. He could put an arm around her shoulder and hug her to him, and she would wind her arm around his waist as the cameras ground. But as soon as they moved out of the crowds, she shifted almost imperceptibly under his arm, which he dropped; she moved away, her face composing itself into its normal wary look. Now the President found himself observing the heavy stance of her plump body, set foursquare against her anger and pain, the tension in her neck, or the looks she gave him these days when she said good night, a piercing, questioning glance. She knew something had happened to him. She assumed it concerned another of his easy ladies, affairs thrown in her face.

One night he woke up at the usual four A.M. He opened his eyes to the dim light of the empty room. "Not here," he said aloud, remarking on the absence of that one angelic image that now tugged always at his mind. Behind his eyes rose memories. It is impossible to get to the monarchy without having performed Aztec sacrifices, and lying there, alone and unprotected, he was assailed by his own betrayals.

How many deaths had he dealt out? Most frequently it is the human heart we kill—ambitions or love or the creative instinct. But he was head of state, and the blood of living men and women lay on him as well. His policies, his acts, affected everyone. Nursing homes and nursery schools, food, transportation, business opportunities—all the stuff of living and dying was in his hands.

"I never meant to harm," he cried aloud, and suddenly he was walking with Anne, hand in hand, across a college campus under the falling red maple leaves. "You watch. I'm going to be President," he announced. Her head was thrown back, eyes sparkling as she looked at him. He'd not thought of that in years. Or of their first two-room apartment, when he was still in law school and held a night job on the side, while Anne, then pregnant, worked at the university. They hardly had time to meet, against opposing schedules, and when they did, could barely tear themselves apart. The passing years were marked by larger apartments and houses, and moves from his home state to Congress (a house in Georgetown), to Governor (the mansion in the home-state capital), and each move took something out of Anne, though she smiled gallantly and made a joke about a rolling stone. In that period she developed a twitch at the corner of her mouth. He wondered if she drank in the afternoons, but had no time to worry about it and bought her a maid instead, and got her a membership in the country club so that she could play tennis or golf with other political wives, and entertain at the club, if need be, and not bother him with her troubles.

It was four-thirty in the morning, and no angel had appeared. His thoughts were lions roaming round their cage. Then—without warning—both his boys pounced on him, and he scrambled to recover his wits, for these were memories he never permitted to himself. Nonetheless they roared onto him: his sons, just little guys, tough and compact of body, not two feet high and swinging at baseballs or flailing at the water when he took them swimming; or later, as adolescents, wrestling one another in the pool with the splashes of whales. They were growing into fine young muscled men; and frantically he tried to jerk his thoughts onto another track—his work, a woman—Eileen, Rebecca—the Peruvian problem to resolve—but they pressed in on him, those two great grinning, awkward, clownish boys with their huge hands and gawky feet, the elder having hardly achieved full height, but taking out girls, starting to drink now and also make speeches in the congressional campaigns, when they took the car for that fatal ride and left their bodies under the tractor trailer on the Beltway, their blood and muscles slippery on the road.

He screamed. The highway smeared with blood.

His heart was pounding. His skin had broken out in sweat.

The door opened. Frank: "Sir?"

"Go away," he growled. "Get out. I'm thinking." But he threw his feet on the cold floor and padded to the angry bathroom to relieve himself, and the tears were running down his unshaven cheeks as he stood before the toilet and pain seared all his joints. His shoulders shook. He could not stop the tears.

Afterward he gulped cold water. He washed his face. He threw himself still trembling back in bed— uncoupled, he was, by his dear dead boys who had taken with them all his love and dried good, lusty ambition into dust.

Instantly he was Anne, scorched by hate at how he'd used their deaths. His teeth began to chatter. He threw off the covers and slipped to his knees beside the bed. "God, help me. Help me," he prayed, as if a deity were not imaginary. "Help me," he prayed. Until suddenly he was kneeling in his imagination at Anne's feet, kissing Anne's feet in love and supplication. But before she could extend forgiveness, the image broke into the figure of the boys, who reached down and hauled him up, enfolded him in their great snuffling embrace, which turned to shoulder-pummeling and leg-wrestling and then to one of those wild racing rough-houses that shook the lamps as they all three thundered from the living room up the stairs and through the bedrooms and down to the basement again, the house rocking with their roars. No cushion was left in place where they had played. Laughing, they threw themselves on the floor.

The vision changed. He was staring at the image of his half-grown sons. They stood before him enveloped in a light beyond imagining, and they weren't doing anything, just standing, looking, smiling at the air.

The President woke from his trance and pulled himself exhausted into bed. He was drained. Now his tears were not for the boys or Anne or even for himself (though God knows he had wept for them before), but for all suffering in this life, this short-lived fragile little life. So fragile, he thought. So fragile that nothing is given us to keep, but only to lose, to lose, to lose.

It seemed to him, lying there with the first pearl light creeping across the sky, that all of life is no more than that adjustment to loss: loss of pets, loss of parents, loss of children, loved ones, loss of homes and dreams. Whatever we value is taken from us. It was intolerable. But then it occurred to him how just this was, how right, how incorruptible, and how our task was merely to accept our loss, and grieve appropriately and give it away, because at some level there is no loss, he thought, hovering on the edge of insight and struggling to hold the idea that was already slipping from consciousness, another loss. For a moment he caught the concept that during our lives we must undergo loss again and again, loss of love, loss of people, loss of possessions, until we lose our possessiveness and see that only with loss is there possibility of . . . and he lost the words as he lost consciousness. It flashed across his mind—there is no loss—before he fell into sleep so sweet that Frank had to shake him awake in the daylight morning, where he lay in bed marveling at his serenity after such a stormy night.

The next morning, he found Anne in the breakfast room, reading her mail through her half-specs and dictating answers to her secretary.

"I saw the boys last night."

She looked up, disgusted. "Oh, Matt."

"Go away," he said to her secretary, seating himself at the table, at which Anne quickly stood.

"Stay, Marie," she ordered. But the secretary had more discretion than her boss.

"I'll wait outside." She slipped away, hearing only Anne's voice rising in annoyance to her husband:

"Really, Matt. Must you?"

"Sit down," he said quietly.

"I don't want to hear your recital."

"I think they came back to say that they're all right."

"Oh, for God's sake!" She paced the room in agitation, pulling at her ring.

"Annie, it was all right. I saw them, I tell you. They stood in front me, both boys, looking at me so lovingly. They were happy."

"You're such an egoist, Matt. I cannot imagine why—"

"Annie, they came to tell us something."

"Then tell them to come to *me*," she said. Then in a burst of frustration, "How could you do this to me? How dare you? I am sick of this charade. I will not put up with it anymore. You have your presidency. You have what you wanted. Glory. Power. So live with it. But don't come to me with your guilty conscience."

"Goddamn it, Anne. I didn't kill them."

"You might as well have. And if not them, then all the other boys you're killing in this war."

"Goddamn you!"

"I do my business. Just don't ask anything more of me, understand?" They faced each other eye to eye, before he turned on his heel and left, muttering about murder and wives.

8

So the days passed into weeks as the planet raced ever faster toward the sun, picking up speed as it approached the finish line (the January ought-three perihelion, when, closest to the sun, it turned and began the long and slowing journey away from its focal star). Some people believed the days were growing shorter because Daylight Savings Time had ended, and others, more learned, because of the tilt of the autumn Earth; but time had no place in those later days. The President felt he only just got up in the morning and turned around once before it was time to fall back in bed. Time took no pause. He felt breathless as the year was running out, as if he were the figurehead of a ship on the soaring planet Earth, and it was running at 1,663,929 miles a day toward the sun, which was itself sweeping through space at some unimaginable velocity; and the solar winds were roaring through Matt's hair, so that if he didn't hold on, he would be blown right off the surface of the Earth into the nothingness of space.

So he held on and did his job and grinned and played the game.

But the President had a secret, and the secret was his connection with the beggar in the park.

As with all secrets, the owner guarded it jealously. He would not reveal his obsession, but he fingered it in meetings or while jogging on his exercise machine, or during the massage afterward, soothed by the caresses of his masseur. He found himself glancing out the window toward the park as he walked down the corridor with his aides, and always in the evening, as he prepared for bed, he found some opportunity to stroll to the north window casually and glance outside, looking for the demonstrators in the empty park.

It was Jim who noticed that the single vagrant was back; he asked the President if he wanted the man removed. He was not a protestor and therefore, technically, did not belong with the dissident group that had been rounded up earlier. Sometimes he sat cross-legged on a park bench, sometimes he stretched on his blanket on the grass. Sometimes he went away, and then for hours at a stretch—or days—he would be gone. Should he be removed?

Matt cut in quickly. "No, no, just leave him there, no harm."

One reason was the craftiness the President had developed: He didn't want to seem more eccentric than Jim probably already found him. But the other reason was because the man in the park, this derelict, belonged to him. He watched him from the window on the second floor. He made inquiries. The man apparently was sane. Not troublesome. Or quarrelsome. But Matt, the sensitive, knew this anyway.

The President took to walking to the front gate of the mansion—for exercise, he said. He waved to the tourists, shaking hands (to the dismay of the secret service) through the iron fence, and letting himself be photographed, happily bantering with the crowd. Then he shot a look at the park, looking for the vagrant, wondering if he noticed. Sometimes the beggar was in the park and sometimes not. When he was there, the President felt a surge of triumph, a vindication of some sort, mingled with antagonism and rage. When he was not, he felt a sag of disappointment. Then he stalked irritably back to the White House, to his office, his desk, his papers and meetings and international crises, and threw himself into life and death.

One night in December a fine sleet slashed at the windows. The President stood with his back to the fireplace and a brandy in his hand. It was eleven o'clock. He could not keep the image from his mind. It had risen before him during the rare, private dinner with his wife, at which they talked like strangers before the servants or lapsed into their private prolonged silences. He did not know what she thought about in such moments—the boys, her trips, her work, perhaps her lover in California. His own thoughts were interrupted by the beggar, whose figure retreated later in the face of the papers he was studying; but when Anne had nodded good night and gone to her room, when he had started a snifter of brandy, the soft, sharp aroma floating in his nostrils and swirling around his tongue, then the man's presence crept out from the back of his brain again, demanding his attention. He rang his butler and gave the order.

A few minutes later two marines jogged through the sleet, weapons at port arms and puttees flashing white, down to the White House gate, across Pennsylvania Avenue and into the wet park. They stopped before the beggar, sitting blanketed on the bench. Their uniforms were drenched. One on either side, they marched him quickstep to the Presidential Palace.

He met them at the door, two dripping marines at smart salute flanking a short and dirty, ragged, bearded, wet rat of a man. Undistinguished. Middle-aged. A blanket covered his shoulders, sending up the heavy smell of wet wool. Matt looked directly at no one.

"Take him to the kitchen. See that he is given something to eat. Get something for yourselves. Frank." He turned to his valet. "See that they have what they need. As for this man." He gestured idly. "Give him some dry clothes and bring him to my study."

He turned away before the others did. Waiting, he felt a thrill of excitement. He had no idea what he would say to the man or what he wanted from him. For the moment he was satisfied to have brought the beggar in. He congratulated himself that his charity was guarding the man from the elements, that he was having him dried and fed. Not even a dog, a horse, is left outdoors, he thought, without a shed. He rubbed his hands before the fire, then turned his back to it, surveying the richness of his room.

Frank knocked, and at the President's order, opened the door to let the beggar in, then stood politely to one side. The vagrant looked a different man. He was dressed in a clean white shirt and a pair of the President's old brown slacks, only moderately too big. He had showered. His beard was hastily clipped. Matt forced his muscles to relax. He realized he was hungry for this man to make a first false move—break wind or shy under the sofa crazily, spit on the Oriental rug, perhaps, or maybe even spring at his throat. Glory and a footnote in history books belong to the crackpots who take potshots at a President.

Yet this man stood before him calmly, with no evidence of servility. Moreover, he showed no lack of ease.

This wordless exchange had occurred in the time it took to blink, and the President was aware of his own annoyance.

"Do you like it?" He waved one hand around the room. "Sit down. Some drinks please, Frank."

"Sir. You shouldn't be alone with—"

"This gentleman is too wise to make an unnecessary move."

"Sir, the secret service would—"

"Do as I say. What would you like? Scotch? Cognac?"

"Hot chocolate would be nice," the beggar said. The man had a pleasant voice, relaxed, not at all what Matt expected.

"Don't you want a drink?" he asked, surprised. "I have a good cognac here. Or perhaps a glass of vodka? You can have anything." He was testing the man. He wanted to make him drunk.

"Chocolate with marshmallow, if you have it. And perhaps I'll put in a dollop of brandy," said the other, leaning back in the sofa. "Usually I don't drink."

"Never?"

"But I'd like something hot now. It's cold out there."

"Chocolate," Frank repeated. He left the door open when he left. The President could see a sentry stationed respectfully six feet beyond the door, and suddenly he wondered who the prisoner was. It had never occurred to him before. He turned back to his guest.

The vagrant was observing him with a strangely steady stare. He neither spoke nor moved.

Matt sank into a chair. He cut short a desire to point out his possessions, the beauty of the pictures on the walls, the colorful cushions, the antique rug. "Did they feed you well in the kitchen?"

"I thank you." He half rose, gave a modest bow,

and settled back on the couch as gracefully as an English lord, though more slovenly, being in clothes a size too big. He gave a little tug at his pants at the knees. He crossed one leg. And slapped both hands on his thighs. "It's very kind of you to take an interest in me." He smiled up at the President sweetly. It's a challenge, Matt thought.

"I have no interest," he said. The lie hung between them in the room. He rose and turned away to stab at the fire roughly with the poker. "I don't like to see men suffer needlessly." Then suddenly he burst out: "Why do you sit out there? What do you get from it? Night, day, rain, snow. Are you mad? Staring at the White House. What the hell do you think you're trying to prove?" He was waving the poker at his guest.

"Does it bother you?"

"Why didn't you stay in the shelter?" When he replaced the poker in its stand and wiped his palms on a handkerchief, he saw his hands were shaking. He thrust them in his pockets. But he could hardly control his voice. "Why? I had you all moved there. They feed you, take care of you. Give you medical care. That's what you want, isn't it? To be picked up and cared for? So you don't have responsibility for anything at all? Not even for yourself?" He stopped himself. His outburst was undignified.

Moreover he knew the street people, the dispossessed, were often sick with drink or drugs. Or else they were mentally unstable, sometimes outright insane. There was no way they could take care of themselves.

The two men stared at one another. The silence lengthened. The President saw the man was not so old as he had first surmised. His hair was grizzled, his beard a brindled red and gray. His skin was weathered with a fine tracery of good-humored wrinkles at the corners of the eyes. He could be anywhere from forty-five to sixty, Matt thought. His eyes were arresting, the color of charcoal splashed with light.

"You're obviously healthy." Matt broke the silence again, this time more calmly. He paced to the silver cigarette box on his desk and offered it to his guest. The beggar shook his head.

"You're not stupid. Why don't you do something useful with your life, earn your way, instead of asking to be taken care of?"

"I'm not asking to be taken care of," said the man.

"You sit out there in all weather." The President closed the silver box with a snap and replaced it on the desk. He sipped his drink. "What's your name?" The question carried a command.

"Gabe."

"Gabe." The President laughed.

"Short for Gabriel. Romantic mother. You can call me Bill. Some people call me Bill."

The President was hardly listening. "No last name? You don't even have a name?"

"I do."

Suddenly the President could not remember why he had invited the man inside. Fury rose in him. He wanted to strangle the man. He could feel his own hands around the vagrant's thick and sinewy neck, fingers fighting the soft tissues of the windpipe which, segmented like a lobster tail, would snap beneath his grip.

He turned away. "How low, how little are the proud, how indigent the great." The lines went through his mind unasked. Who had said that?

"Why didn't you stay in the shelter?" he asked again. "We set it up for you. You're protesting poverty, aren't you? Greed. Your government's uncaring attitude. Well? We provided for your needs."

"I had to get back to work."

"Work!" It was a sneer of contempt. "What? Sitting on a sidewalk?"

"I guess it looks like that." He smiled shyly.

At that moment Frank reappeared with a tray of drinks and mixers and one cup. He poured from the china chocolate pot and offered the cup to the beggar together with sugar and a spoon.

The President poured another brandy in his snifter, and out of spite poured one also for this guest who did not want a drink. He'd had more than enough, but no holds were barred now, not even against himself.

"That's all, Frank. Shut the door behind you." He sipped his drink, and felt the flow of burning relaxation deep in his stomach.

This time the butler made no protest. The door closed with a click.

"Well, what is your work?" challenged the President

with an evil grin. "What do you do all day, sitting there?"

The beggar sipped his chocolate, eyes closed, cupping it with both hands in delicious gratitude—like a child, Matt thought, quite totally absorbed in cocoa.

"I'm sending light."

"Light," repeated the President, with a laugh. That was more like it . . . loony.

"Some people call them prayers."

"What do you mean?" The hair rose on the back of his neck. The President knew about lasers, and some of the more secret weapons of his military.

"I'm protecting you with light. I'm sending light."

The President's laugh was a harsh bark. "You surround me with light?" The man seemed oblivious to his surroundings. Or to Matt, who began to tremble suddenly; his hands were shaking again. "And exactly how do you do that?" he asked, forcing himself to stay calm.

"It can be done, you understand, from a distance. But proximity helps. Why do you think I'm here?"

"Here?" asked the President like a stunned ox.

"In this room. I sent you the suggestion to ask me in. You need my help."

The President stared at the man, aghast. His face went white. Then he took two steps to the door. "Frank!" It was the bellow of a bull. The door burst open to reveal the valet, and behind him, two secret servicemen and a marine. "Get this man out of here.

Take him to the park—shelter. No—to jail. I want him put away."

"On what charge?"

"I don't give a good goddamn. Here!" The President leapt forward to thrust the antique glass paperweight on the desk into the visitor's jacket pocket. "Stealing. Get him out! Get out!" he shouted. "And keep him away. He's not to come close, do you hear?"

But when the door closed on the beggar, on Frank, on the three palace guards, the President inexplicably fell on his knees and pounded the coffee table with his fist, though why—what constituted his frustration—he did not know. He wanted the beggar back again. He had forgotten to ask him about the angel. He wanted no more of the whole business.

Everything was confusion for Matt Adams: insecurity, doubt, fear.

"Oh, God!" he groaned. "Oh help." He wished he were a little boy again in the warm kitchen of his grandmother's house, and she, his mother's mother, would be taking Toll House cookies out of the oven (the warm smell of chocolate), and he would sit, legs dangling, his chair tucked close to the table, eating warm cookies and sipping his cocoa—

Cocoa!

He caught his breath. The beggar had drunk hot chocolate.

He tossed his cognac down his throat, set down the glass, and started out the door to bed, striding fast to run away from the pursuing thoughts. For one terrifying moment he didn't know if he was the beggar or the President, the child or man.

He plunged into his bedroom and stopped. His heart was pounding. There. He was the President. Back in his body again. His clothes were laid out on the bed. He could hear Frank in the bathroom turning on his shower. How did the man know when he was coming? Eyes in the back of his head. He was the President, but for one awful moment it had seemed quite reasonable that he was the beggar instead, sitting on a park bench sending vibrations to the White House. Or destitute. Indigent. And dreaming of being President.

In all his life Matt had never had that sense of not being himself, of being outside himself.

He was an only child. He'd wanted to be noticed, he remembered. His father had left, and his mother was working—it was one of the depression cycles—first in a retail store, and later in a lawyer's office, so Matt didn't see her much.

He lived in a small town. Sagging brick buildings. Abandoned warehouses. If he hadn't been an athlete, on scholarship to the university, he'd never have gotten out.

But he'd always known he wouldn't stay. He wanted to be loved, yes, and to win; if he couldn't be loved, at least he could win, and then he'd be admired and respected, loved.

He had no trouble making friends. Always in a pack, leader of the pack, and the mud sliding they did and pounding down alleys, and screaming, playing with swords or wrestling with each other, rough and tumble and a lot of physical activity. And then the way of it—the girls. The girls would walk past and the boys would go quiet for a second, as if a monster had passed (they were only ten or twelve) and then erupt into screams and shouts, catcalls, and they'd jump and push each other wildly, and run like crazy, running away from the girls and running toward them, showing off. And the girls in their ankle socks, carrying schoolbooks, would turn their imperious heads and sniff. Or else, sometimes, collapse into giggles themselves and run away.

And later, in high school, he fell in love every third week, they were all so pretty. Betty and Nancy and Mary Lee. He had one girl, Lucy, and they necked and kissed and explored each other's bodies in ways his mother would have beat him for if she'd known.

One day he heard his father had died, this father whom he had never met. He called Lucy and took her out into the woods behind the school and kissed her fiercely. He felt her breasts and put his hand up her skirt, while she squirmed and twisted in delicious horror, as his hand went up into her underpants.

"Stop," she whispered. "I'll get pregnant." He felt angry. He was hot, a demon then, and he came all over her, pumping himself clean between her frightened legs, and when he got up from the woodsy, earth-smelling forest floor, he stood looking down at her. He was a man! He wanted to crow. But she burst into tears. She kept smoothing her dress with tight little gestures and looking at him with aggrieved eyes. "Why did you do that?" she asked again and again—as if he had done something to her. And, "There's a stain on my dress. What will my mother say?"

He didn't care what her mother said. Suddenly he disliked Lucy. He held out his hand, though, and pulled her to her feet and put one arm around her and told her everything would be all right. And walked her to the corner where she lived. He left her. He went to his room in his own house and jerked off. Afterward, she began to talk about marriage.

He left town. And he never went back except for his mother's funeral, that was all, and for the unveiling of the memorial they put up for him, favorite and most famous son. He started college and then his political career and left that sad little ragged childhood behind.

Everyone voted for him in his hometown. They claimed him now, and now he couldn't do wrong by them in that place.

So what is life about? Why was he not happy? He had everything he'd ever wanted, and the goddamn pols worrying that he was not pursuing war. He kept thinking about the past—about Randolph, who'd been his best friend in sixth grade. Randy became a dentist, and he was dead too; and Don, who drove a truck till he retired, and now he drove a motorboat; and Jervey Moffett and Beth and Bev, and they were all gone mostly, and he himself President, the most important man in the world, who had indulged in sex with countless women, whose faces and names he couldn't recall. And here he was thinking about Lucy. And what was life about? He didn't have any idea at all.

It was a strange world in those days, with chaos and destruction everywhere. The prince of one country killed 150 soldiers, all by himself, point-blank, a bullet to the back of the head. Chaos and chemical war, and the Ring of Fire waiting for us all. And in each human being a mind so magnificent that every one of us holds a universe, complete and separate; and such order in this chaos that the moon swings full across the sea of night like a God every twenty-eight to thirty days. That's chaos there? *The chaos is inside of me*, he thought, *in me*.

He kept thinking about Lucy, who'd married Randy, actually, and they'd had four children and she was a good mother and she was happy with him and he with her before he died. They never wanted anything they didn't have or couldn't get.

While Matt had always wanted more. So he was President, and still it wasn't enough.

Only now he was responsible not for the boys in the backyard alley wars, but for the whole world. And do you know? He felt he didn't know a thing.

That night he dreamt he was living in a tin shanty, as did three-quarters of the people of the world in those days. He was Monarch of the World, but he couldn't do anything about the slums, and he too was living barefoot in an alley, a beggar, and dying at a furious, fast pace.

9

One night the President stood before the mirror in the bathroom, peering at his tired eyes. He looked worn. He covered his face with his hands before the mirror, then dashed them down in a vain attempt to catch his image in the glass. But only the mask of his face stared back, blue eyes probing. He turned around, then swung back quickly to the mirror to see if he could catch the man who hid behind his eyes.

You can see how troubled he was.

An angel had appeared. But what had it done? What had it said? An angel was supposed to be a messenger, and all he knew was that it had come and looked at him compassionately, and left him for a beggar. Whatever that meant. The President was caught by the terror that life was more meaningful than he was prepared to accept, and by the horror that it might not be. He was frightened by the responsibility implied.

He still talked to himself.

"Listen, God," he said fiercely. "You listen to me. You're not doing so good a job down here. What can we expect from a God who is jealous and vain? You're not good enough, you hear? God shield us, anyway"—he turned away—"from the love of God." Who'd want that love? Look what He did to his Best Beloved Only Begotten Son—tortured, murdered, hung with thieves—or St. Peter crucified upside down; and the other early martyrs, shipwrecked and imprisoned, torn limb from limb, eaten by lions, shot with arrows, castrated and mutilated, the women's breasts cut off, and little children slain. Or, God help us, to the Chosen People! Chosen by God for diaspora and holocaust. Better to be ignored by God than win that kind of love.

"Haven't you any shame?" he called out in the night. "What father would give his child a stone when he asks for bread? Go away," he muttered to himself. "Go away. Take care of other planets. I have no place for God."

Another time: "I don't believe in your angel. I reject a spirit world that meddles in our everyday affairs."

He wanted nothing to do with God, the celestial psychopath.

And yet the angel had come, not once but twice, sent him a wave of love and left him radiant with joy.

He used two tricks of mind, therefore, to get himself off the hook. Either the angel, he decided, had come to him because he was the President, a statesman, a man of power doing a good job, as it were, and come to congratulate him perhaps, or give encouragement. Or else he disbelieved in the event.

But no sooner did that thought take root than he remembered the angel's eyes, the rapturous leap of his heart on looking into them. He wanted more. He brooded. If an angel had come to him, then why not a troop of angels at Auschwitz? Or in the Middle East?

And why, if it came for comfort, did it leave him in this wilderness? He, the President, who had never bothered about epistemological matters before; he, Matt, the problem solver, who had become with the visitation as displaced as a vagrant, full of passions and guilt; and never in his life had he been so vulnerable to pain. It was as if a layer of skin had been torn off him, his heart exposed. That's what the President found; and never had he felt more prey to doubt.

At the time the angel appeared, the world was burning up.

It was in all the daily news: earthquakes and typhoons and people swept away in tidal waves, and

whole towns and villages buried by volcanic erup-
tions or mud slides formed in heavy rain; and there
was starvation and famine—bone-deep hunger in the
face of plenty—and children born deformed and
crippled, and young people suffering from disease,
and lovers being killed, or husbands falling in love
with other women, or wives with other men, and the
elderly dying alone and incontinent and often in
great humiliation and pain. You did not need to look
far to find suffering in this world.

Some people denied the existence of God on the
basis of this suffering alone; and others were subject
to a religious fervor that broke over the nation in
those days, and still others drowned their terror in
open promiscuity or drugs, dancing in the Vanity
Fair; for terror was stalking everyone, and especially
at the prospect of being snuffed out at any time without warning—or maybe even worse, *with* warning—
and never seeing the sunlight again.

Now there were also people who accepted these
horrors as the downside of the best of all possible
worlds, and enjoyed themselves anyway, heads up,
with a smile on their lips. But the despairing ones
agreed that such people were insensitive, that attention must be paid to these things, attention must be
paid.

Among this group was the journalist Jake Bauer.
His business was to find out everything going on in
the White House and Government and to spread it

like manure at the feet of what was called the People. To fertilize their imaginations.

Jake was thirty-nine years old. Cynical, tough, athletic, he had quick, slashing gestures and an aggressive voice. He expected the worst of people and was rarely disappointed. He hated Authority, especially over him.

He thought the world was not behaving as it should (which is to say according to his wishes), and that the only hope lay in the Rule of Law. Only a constant surveillance could prevent wrong-doing. As a good reporter, he opposed Government, which he saw as always ready to teeter into a police state, totalitarianism, dictatorship: He opposed any tightening of the reins of order. On the other hand, he also opposed the intellectual disorder of States' Rights, the private power of international Corporations (fiefdoms in their own right), and any other efforts at the dispersal of authority. What he did believe in (and it was this that led him to call himself an optimist) was Balance of Power, or Law. The two Empires were checked by the Balance of Power; Corporations by laws of States; individual States by the central Government, the central Government by a vigilant Press—which was to say, himself.

If Jake had had his way, this Rule of Law would have worked in the same effortless way that planets swing in perpetual motion, never falling from their silent, spellbound paths. It annoyed him that human affairs drifted messily, and his frustration spurred him to work harder to compensate.

There were two or three explanations of what purpose the diligent altruism of a Free Press served.

Idealists claimed that the People had a Right to Know, and that the Light of Public Scrutiny, or an informed citizenry, or the threat of public shame, kept the politicians straighter (or less crooked, at least) than they otherwise might be.

But cynics called it gossip, and merely an excuse for advertising, so that media owners could dine on good meats and fine wines. The news, after all, was by definition bad—a dose of depression to make people buy something to make them feel good again.

The politicians, themselves, often felt the Press were wolves snarling at their heels. Every now and again they threw the wolves a hunk of meat or even one of their own, and raced toward safety across the tundra in their troikas; while behind them the Press snapped and grabbed hungrily at the carcass before lifting their heads with a terrible howl and turning to the scent again. Matt felt this as well, though he tried to remember that the Fourth Estate served a purpose in the scheme of Democracy, that the Press acted in a kind of partnership with him, especially when he could manipulate it. There were times when he was ready to damn the Fourth Estate and hated the People anyway, their only saving grace being that they often had more interest in the crossword puzzle, sports, and entertainment than in any news that Jake and his compatriots were inclined to give.

The President distrusted Jake. He would have distrusted him even more had he known that for the past few months the journalist had been sniffing out a story about the demonstrators in the park, and that he had dug out of one secretary a curious interest of the President's in these dispossessed people, who were now the wanderers.

At the next press conference Jake shot to his feet. "Mr. President!"

Matt tensed for Jake's next effort to embarrass him.

"Mr. President, is it true you invited a tramp into your private quarters last week?"

The President's jaw dropped.

"What's your relationship to this man, and have you known him long?" asked Jake, stabbing at the President with one finger. "Is it true that he's now in jail?"

A murmur ran round the room. No one had heard the story yet. Matt thought fast on his feet. He gave his engaging laugh and turned his charm like a searchlight on Jake.

"I see there's nothing private in the presidency." Which made Jake glow with pride. "Yes, I did invite one of the homeless of this city, a street person, into the White House. It was a private act, as a private citizen. My own investigative reporting, you could say. Unfortunately, he stole an antique paperweight.

As for jail, I can't say. I don't know what happened to him," he lied.

"What about the paperweight? Was it recovered?"

"What made you choose this man?"

"Are you planning to invite in other street people? Is this going to be a practice?"

But Jake gave a wolfish grin, for he had verification of what he'd found. That night every paper in the country and all the TV news reported it, but Jake's story was the most detailed. He pranced around the newsroom, boasting openly of his scoop. His story told of a derelict who sat yogi-fashion either in Lafayette Park or else on the Ellipse, always facing the White House, like a Muslim to Mecca; and of how the President had paid him the courtesy of his attention one rainy night; how the prince and the pauper had talked intimately, long into the night, as cats can talk to kings; of how the President had fed and clothed him and let him spend the entire stormy night on the white linen of a warm, dry White House bed; and finally how, on leaving, it was discovered the beggar had stolen a valuable eighteenth-century paperweight. Perhaps other things as well.

That's the story Jake told, only slightly off the facts.

Jake first criticized the President for putting himself in a vulnerable position, unprotected from a possible attack, then questioned the government version of the street person being a thief, and finally the competence of the police; for apparently the beggar had now mysteriously disappeared. Jake had confirmation of that fact. Police records showed his name, the crime—and then the beggar had walked out of his cell, to vanish without a trace.

The first Matt heard that the man had disappeared was over his morning coffee, as he read Jake's story. The paperweight had also disappeared. Irritating.

The President received letters and telegrams from all over the country, some applauding his hospitality, others critical that he had invited a vagrant into his home, which was also public property and not to be abused. Some expressed heartfelt concern for the President's safety, and others suggested he could do more; use the downstairs White House rooms, for example, as a shelter for the homeless and indigent. Still others spat out their hatred of the poor and ill, and urged their elimination from the world.

The publicity annoyed the President as much as the part he'd played in the little drama—sending an innocent man to jail. But he had little attention to give the situation. The world was breaking over him, and he had no time to waste. He tried to remind himself that everything is relative, and all he had was time and the choice of how to use it best.

Around him, strange things were happening. Abroad, the Premier of the Eastern Empire was rumored to be ill, though no one knew with what. Rumors flew:

Dissidents jailed;

Ordinary people killed, their brains blown out with guns, and their blood splattering, spattering on the beautiful earth;

And cries of mourning everywhere.

At home, the homeless lived like animals in Rock Creek Park, in caves, in boxes, in the hollows of fallen trees, and some of them formed robber bands, kicked ass, frightened the homeful who avoided the savagery in their midst.

On the border, the Barbarians were said to be massing. More war news. Only it was nothing new. The news would be if no one were fighting either there or in the other sixty-three locations on the globe.

At the center of the universe, out in the silence of utter space, scientists discovered a Black Hole, hundreds of thousands of light-years wide. Now, that was something to fear. It sucked with its enormous gravity at the rest of the universe. Meanwhile the physicists were watching irrational and playful subatomic particles jump like circus fleas. Here was the question for the scientists: Was all this, too, an expression of the love that moves the sun and stars?

Back at home it was Christmas. Then, for the third time, the angel appeared.

10

At Christmas the presidential family traditionally held a large gathering for the politicians, White House staff, and the Press. One of those invited was Jake, who brought his little daughter, Lily, to view the Christmas tree.

Jake was divorced and saw Lily only on weekends, and sometimes not even then if he had work to do. Since he loved her more than anyone on earth, he was pleased to show off to her at Christmas the palace where he worked.

Fifty other children were there too, dressed in party clothes and eyeing on tiptoe the platters of sweets and cakes and candied orange peel as the grown-ups bellowed at each other from three feet above. In one corner stood a group of carolers dressed in red velvet, and in another stood the tree with false packages all gaily wrapped and heaped around its foot. The smells of ginger and nutmeg hung in the air; the crowd was thick enough to make it hard for the waiters to push through with their trays of hot wine or platters of oysters and cheese canapés; and when the double doors opened to show the banquet table laden with hams and turkeys and nuts and cheeses and fish and fruits and cakes and chocolates, you could hear the sigh of pleasure; and then the moving feet, the crush, as the assembled guests shouldered through the doorway to descend on the table like the locusts on Egypt and clean off every tray. In no time the platters were reduced to ragged tails and scraps, limp parsley and sagging sculptured Santas of vegetables and candied fruit, as if the crowd had never eaten before. Waiters replenished the platters, running in and out with trays.

In the midst of this happy throng, several hundred strong, the President, quite his old self now—recovered from his madness, it seemed, or stroke or hallucinations—mingled, first with his wife on his arm doing her duty as First Lady, then separately, each working the crowd like well-trained bird dogs, and whenever possible dropping first-name benisons on their friends.

The President shook hands with the Episcopal bishop and made a point of greeting the tall, bald, Fundamentalist minister who had been invited to counterbalance the bishop, and of course in honor of the season; and he spoke to a black Baptist minister and a white rightist, and a Supreme Court justice, and many other important personages who were celebrating the idea of tolerance and mercy on that holiday.

Matt was also pleased to see that Jim Sierra had brought his wife Susan and their two girls. Christmas—Hanukkah—this darkest period of the northern year—is a time of reconciliation, when fighting couples vow once more to make their marriages work. The President greeted Susan warmly, strangely grateful that she had taken her husband back, even if it was for the children's sake; and he laughed with her about the phone call he had made, and listened to her awkward stuttered apologies with a certain prideful satisfaction. Around him the voices rose in a deafening din, and the musicians played, and the carolers sang, and the Christmas tree lights winked among gaudy velvet-ribboned balls.

The President could not possibly have noticed Lily, elbow-high to the guests and twisting past their hips, drawn for reasons she could not ascertain to the edge of the room, where she stopped short; for there stood an angel, and in all that crowd no one brushed against its radiance.

She stood, rapt, watching it shimmer and glow. It was formed of a wonderful whiteness, more brilliant than any whiteness of this earth, and yet it flared with colors too; it had no wings, and yet it gave an impression of pinions, for the light of which it was composed flowed up and down, in and out, like breathing, leaving an impression like the waving of wings.

The angel stood alone, smiling at the crowd, and Lily held her breath. Then it turned and smiled at her. She waved one tentative hand. "Hello," she whispered. But her voice was lost in the singing, which flooded everything. It was like nothing she had ever heard before (though later Jake disputed this: The noise was only the musicians playing on the far side of the room). So they stood a moment, the angel and the little child of wondrous innocence, and then Lily moved closer to the figure, which bent toward her, responding to her silent question. At which she threw herself at its feet.

Matt saw a surging of the guests, a shifting like sand toward one corner of the room. A child had fainted.

"What's happened?"

The child had dropped to the floor, feet under her, and was staring idiotically at the wall, crying uncontrollably. Jake, frightened, embarrassed, pushed through to her side.

"Get up, Lily. Don't crumple on the floor." He pulled her arm.

"Yes," she murmured.

"Well, do it! What's wrong?" Her legs were noodles.

"Do you see it, Daddy?" she said, making no effort to stand. "Look."

"Lily, get up." The angel faded at this moment and a wail rose from Lily's throat.

"Lily! Stop it."

"It's gone. Did you see it? Daddy, did you look?"

"See what?"

"It was an angel."

The Fundamentalist minister stopped to overhear. He was a tall thin man, an Ichabod Crane, the President thought, a Giacometti, a setter dog on point. Then everything happened at once, a flurry of activity. Matt, approaching, thought the child was sick. He saw Jake standing over her, as well as the tall, lean, balding and black-coated minister, and each was tugging on one arm. Jake was ordering his daughter to stand up, and the minister to describe what she had seen.

"Let go," she cried to both.

"What is it?" said the guests, and, "What's happening?"

"A miracle!" cried the minister. His voice could fill a cathedral without a microphone, and he liked to try. "It's an angel! This innocent child has seen an angel! There's an angel here."

The President felt sick. He put one hand against the wall, while the room revolved.

"Take your hands off her," said Jake, pushing at the strange minister in black, who fought back angrily. It was the preacher's territory, after all, and Jake, though father to the child, was trespassing.

" 'And a little child shall lead them,' " he boomed in his carrying voice. "Tell us what you see, girl."

Lily's voice wailed above them all, a treble siren.

"Great balls of fire!" said the Episcopal bishop at the President's elbow. His mouth curled with contempt.

"Out of the mouths of babes!" cried the Fundamentalist. "On your knees, O ye faithless," he continued, following his own direction in his enthusiasm. "There's an angel in our midst!"

"Stop that maniac," ordered the President through gritted teeth to no one in particular.

"Jesus said, 'Suffer the little children to come unto—'" But the rest of his words were lost in the babble of the crowd. Such is the fate of a prophet in his own land.

Jake was pulling on his daughter, folding his child into his protective embrace. "Let go!" he snarled at the minister, who, still kneeling, folded his long body, legs of a heron, down toward Lily; and she lay curled in a ball on the floor—an armadillo, a hedgehog—covering her head with the fluttering hands and arms that the two men tried to pry apart.

The President pushed forward. "Let me through," he ordered, and the people fell back respectfully, so that he managed to put one hand on Jake's arm just as he was drawing back to slug the minister.

"Hey, Jake." As if addressing a horse, calmingly, soothingly. He held the father's shoulder momentarily, then leaned down to pick up Lily, and, because he was President, the other two relinquished their ambitious holds.

"You get this bastard away from my daughter." Jake's eyes burned with rage.

"It's a miracle!" cried the minister again, still carried away by the event, though dampened by uneasiness, for perhaps she had seen nothing and was fooling everyone. If so, it was too late: He had placed his bets when he first opened his mouth; he could not renege. "She saw an angel, Mr. President. An angel in this very room, right at Christmastime."

"Shut up," said the President in annoyance. Then, "Did you?" he asked softly, lifting the child in his arms.

I wish I could say that for one moment he was face-to-face with this enchanting child. She was five, almost six, with an air of such innocent, clear wonder, lips parted, that he could not prevent a smile. But that's not what happened. It was awful. He took her in his arms—all elbows, knees, and joints. A President, an Oriental satrap, is accustomed to respect, not a squirming, slippery, twisting five-year-old slithering out of his arms! He grinned valiantly at the surrounding guests, and almost slung her into her father's grip, where she buried her face in his rough woolen jacket and wept.

Humiliated, Matt patted her gently on the back and turned to laugh at the assembled guests, and was now struck by the silence in the place, for the musicians had stopped playing too, and the crowd had hushed.

"Well, it's good news." He laughed lightly, including the Fundamentalist in his banter. "Any angel's welcome. We could use a host of angels here, protecting us in these times. I've seen lots of angels myself," he said with a mad, deceitful grin that devastated his admirers and broke them into little puffs of laughter.

"That's what Christmas is about—Good Tidings, Peace among us all. So lift your glasses and join me in a toast." He paused to look around and ascertain the mood had broken. "To Peace," he said, with his drink lifted toward the ceiling so all could see. "To the end of the wars. To our collected friends, to Christmas, and to winning the next election."

It was the last phrase that caused the outburst of applause. A shout of approval filled the room and fists were raised high and closed palms with the two-finger V, and voices too, as the musicians struck up the election song.

The President leaned over to Jake. "Take her to my office," he said. "I'll meet you there. I'll get Jim Sierra to show you."

"I'm taking her home, Mr. President," said the reporter. "Come on, honey. We're going home."

"Don't leave, don't leave," cried the Fundamentalist preacher, rising on tiptoe, a flamingo now as his face flushed red with emotion. "Who are you? What's your name?" he asked the child, who turned her face again, sheltering in her father's lapels.

"Take her to my office," the President ordered, waving Jim up to his side. He didn't want to let her out of his sight any more than the minister did. And now a curious thing occurred. Jake, who would have cut off his fingertip for five minutes alone in the President's office, entirely forgot his work.

"No. We're going home." Brusquely, angrily, he picked her up and pushed through to the hallway, where he snatched their coats from the checkroom and, holding coats as well as Lily in his arms, strode off.

There was nothing the President could do.

Outside the snow fell on an empty Ellipse. Inside, the First Lady smiled at constituents and wished her headache would go away, or that she had time to dream of her lover in California. She had not been in the room when the little girl had fainted, had not understood what the ruckus was about. The Fundamentalist minister attached himself to Jim Sierra, demanding to know the name of the father and child, and then, distracted by reporters, repeated and elaborated on the vision he envisioned she had seen. His deep voice resonated with the words of God. Jim went to the bar to down another drink, and wondered if his wife was sleeping with Jake Bauer, whom he'd seen talking with her, the bitch, in easy intimacy, or if, as she pretended, they'd never met before that night.

And the musicians played and people milled and waiters passed more bottled cheer, which vanished down the open throats.

But Matt Adams, the President, went to his office and sat at his desk, staring out at the dark and empty lawns.

Meanwhile, the world was burning up. The predominant emotion swinging like a comet round the world was . . . fear.

For some people it came as fear of disease or death,

but for many others it was free-floating, like fear of
failure or success. There was fear of not being good
enough (whatever that meant) to make it (whatever
that meant), fear of being found out, or of ridicule or
making a mistake, any one of which would lead to
rejection, isolation, loneliness. So each fear led to
another, but at the root was the fear of separateness,
the terrible isolation of being alone, cast out from
human company. It was a kind of fear of death.
There was fear of economic insecurity, and longing
for a sense of safety, as if money could fill the hollow
of the heart. Some people were afraid of a punitive,
jealous Deity, but few were afraid of losing, or never
finding, grace, though that would constitute the ulti-
mate belonging—oneness, Home!

Almost anything was justified because of fear, but
the world was also burning up with desire; and what
was curious, the most egregious behavior could be
excused, forgiven, if it was caused by fear ("I was so
scared!"), but hardly any act on the grounds of mere
desire ("I wanted it").

Matt wondered, was there any difference between
fear and desire? How do we know when our motives
are pure?

In those days terrible acts were committed,
atrocities, human against human, for everyone was
afraid of pain, and in anxiety created it.

It could be said that the world was burning up
with fear. But hardly anyone noticed that it was also
burning up with joy.

Hardly anyone ran outside in the morning to cry in wonder at the glorious red dawn; or stopped to hail the pale moon scudding through its clouds on coon-hunting night. Hardly anyone gave in to an appropriate, rapt sense of gratitude for the marvel of a cockroach in the kitchen cabinet (product of millennia of breeding true), or the snails under their little shells, eating at the garden lettuce in the spring, or the black-and-brown-striped woolly bears crossing the highways on a crisp fall day, while the geologic plates groaned beneath their tiny, hairy feet and the earth shifted and continents moved and ice caps melted and volcanoes tore through the crust of the earth, erupting in ferocious joy.

There was joy and pleasure even in the suffering, depending on how you decided to view the matter. Even pain and illness comes as a blessing when you consider that its purpose is to warn, to give us a chance to set the matter right. So the world was burning up with joy as well as grief. And babies were being born each hour who were more beautiful than any child before (each mother knew it in her heart). You had only to look at skin like silk and the tiniest of fingernails glued to the ends of dainty fingers, eyes that opened and shut and could focus and discern, and growing limbs, and laughter bubbling from unpretentious throats like pear blossoms in May. Oh! It was a fine, good world in those days, a grand, brave, hearty place to be.

And so were the people who lived in it: children crying to their mothers on a summer's afternoon to

Look! Look at ME! Mom, look! Or the teenagers, struggling with their own brooding, restless, anguished hearts, the growing up and separating from their parents being as painful as for limpets pulled from a seacoast rock. And then the adults, people so old that you'd think nothing further would ever happen in their lives except the toiling, nine to five, and there they were, falling in love, again and again, and making promises they could not keep to love one another for eternity, not remembering that all things change—all hearts, all eyes—and that the only constancy lies in the love of God, which springs up bountifully in our own hearts over and over again, as evidenced by our falling in love like teenagers with lots of different people even up to the age of ninety-two. A fine, good world it was, full of pleasure, if you knew how to look for it in the struggle for shelter and food; full of riches showered on us all. Or full of suffering, if that's what you were happy dwelling on.

The President, lying in bed that night, was struck by the insight. A prayer, he thought, is nothing but a concentrated thought, and if all prayers are answered (as various religions claim) then we constantly create our fate by our own thoughts.

And if we get what we want, he thought, too wide-awake to drop off into sleep, then how can we ever achieve world peace? Humans want thrills, excitement, not serenity; and these are only found in fear.

11

After the party, the President had a new obsession: to see the little girl again. There were things he wanted to ask her. First, he invited her to a private meeting at the White House, to have her picture taken with him, an official photo that he would then sign and give to her as a memento. Photos with presidents were considered of value, like getting your name in the newspaper or your picture on TV. The invitation to Lily was made at the suggestion of the President's secretary, Rosemary, who had children and grandchildren of her own, and therefore knew what would appeal to them.

Jake declined. His regrets were polite and cold. He thanked the President but said he did not want his daughter treated with special favors or to have anything made of the unfortunate incident at the Christmas party, when, due to excitement and exhaustion, she had had an hallucination. He was sure the President would understand. Both he and his former wife were disturbed at the newspaper accounts that had come out about the party. It was embarrassing.

The President's first reaction was anger. He checked his impulse to *order* her to come. The idea passed immediately, the beat of a bat's wings; but he was astonished at the intensity of his rage, disturbed and ashamed. His only course, he advised himself, was patience. Something would happen. The way would be made clear. (He had started to think like this in the last few months, as if Fate were leading him.) Yet impatience drove him on obsessively.

That was another reason he thought he was going mad. At times, he felt all the universe and everyone in it was swinging rightly and righteously in a kind of delicate dance, orderly as a minuet. He could hear the singing of the planets, the humming of rocks and sky; he could comprehend the mathematical movements of the universe—atoms, matter, plants, people, seas and stars, right out to the mystery of millions of galaxies sailing through infinite space.

Then, cupped in a calm hope, he knew he had only to wait. Everything would come to him. These moments of exaltation never lasted long. They were wiped out by events and problems and by his habit of command, an urgency to force a conclusion; or else by doubt, in which he knew with the certainty of despair that nothing was as it appeared, not even his fickle thoughts, and that he knew nothing, nothing at all, and had no control and no strength to effect a single thing. He could not even get his laws through Congress! Then his impulse again was to lunge forward, impose rules, force the situation to its knees. He plotted how to get the child alone.

It was strange. What was supposed to occupy his mind was world depression riding on the tides of war, and the starvation in Africa and Brazil, desperate balance of payments, and the slowly collapsing steel and concrete bridges, the disintegrating roads and subways in his own country, and also the photo opportunities with big contributors, and the reelection of his party.

Instead he tested these private sores. There was still, for example, the matter of the beggar. At night sometimes Matt stared out at the north lawn or prowled from one window to another in the palace, wondering where the man had gone; and why, if his assignment was to help the President, he'd run away. Matt resented the man's absconding with his paperweight, of which, in fact, he was fond. He took it as a betrayal.

I am not fit to rule, he thought; and his advisors, whose advice on this subject he never asked, agreed. They whispered among themselves. They found it unnerving for the President to be concerned about the meaning of life. Humility is not valued in a monarch.

One day he stopped Jim as he was leaving the office, a stack of papers in his arms. "I've been thinking," he said, and Jim paused, respectful to his boss's moods.

"Maybe the only thing that's constant is the changing of either our emotions or our minds," said the President.

"What?"

"It's as if there isn't any reason for living at all except to experience all the emotions, and that that's all we do all day long, have you noticed? Or all week, anyway: anger, fear, joy, sorrow, grief, hate, loneliness, jealousy, happiness. I've been thinking, maybe that's the whole sum of life right there, and all we do is go from one to another, like riding all the horses on a merry-go-round; and maybe all the situations we face are merely tests set before us so that we can experience every emotion in some depth. And try out different answers. What do you think?"

Jim stood in the open doorway a moment, staring at the President, then stepped inside, letting the heavy door close behind him.

"What brought this to mind?" he asked cautiously. He himself had only the most primitive relationship to his own emotions. He wasn't even sure he could name any feeling when he felt it, but he looked at his President, whom he admired more than any human alive, and his mind was racing, searching for the proper response.

"I was thinking how life's a game," said Matt, and he stood up and walked to the window and back and then continued pacing the large oval room as he talked, hands behind his back, thinking aloud on his feet. "It's a game. But why don't we refuse to play? We think the situations we're facing are real, that they *mean* something. We get caught up in our feelings. Or else in *thinking*. That's another trick of the game, that we have to solve these problems. We're always reacting. You'd think we'd get tired of the game, but instead—"

"Are you saying the situations aren't real?" Jim asked in real dismay. Was the President talking about the war? The economic recession? What wasn't real?

"No, they're real, but they're not important. They're ways for us to indulge in all the pleasures and pain that's possible. That's what we want to do. We love it. When we haven't enough excitement in our own lives, we go to the movies to get a jolt. If there's a bit of intellect thrown in, that's okay too. We think the alternative is boredom. We'd rather do something destructive than be bored." He saw Jim's face and flushed.

"Well, of course, to some people the most important thing is intellect—thinking. Or the search for knowledge. They think *what* they're thinking about is important, when it's really only the act of thinking they enjoy, the exercise of the mind; or for another type it's battering the body with physical sensations—the way an athlete does."

He saw Jim's wariness.

"I know. You're thinking the purpose of life is to love thy neighbor," he hurried on, though it couldn't have been further from Jim's mind. "Or to do some good before we die. But most of us just fumble through; it's hard enough just to keep on going."

Jim stared at him appalled.

The President, embarrassed, shifted gears. Even mad he knew he'd revealed too much of his inner thoughts. He gave a laugh, head thrown back. "Don't look like that. Do you think I'm serious?" And he flashed his famous smile and his famous victory sign. "Back to work." And he dismissed his aide.

Jim returned to his own office slowly, his tread muffled on thick carpeting. Around him the aides and officers of the palace hurried here and there. The secret service paced the walkways, talking to each other through the handkerchiefs in their left breast pockets. On guard. Jim shook his head. Was it a joke? He didn't want to think it could be serious. Had he known the extent of Matt's distress it would have troubled him even more.

Matt Adams spent considerable time these days consolidating a new philosophy. He scratched ideas in a notebook at night. The question was: What is reality?

How strange. All his life he'd battled in the public arena. If he examined his soul, it was after a failure, to excuse his behavior or put the blame on someone else; or else to reconsider strategy, for the President was a cunning politician, a user of people and ideas.

Suddenly, his very method of operations was breaking down. He found himself without a center, and he had the discomfiting sensation as he gave a TV talk or flew to Atlanta for a fund-raiser, or met with ambassadors and heads of state, or conferred with the leaders of the Congress and his cabinet, that he was standing outside himself sometimes, watching himself perform.

He was beside himself, you could say.

Here he was, the head of the American Empire, the most powerful man on earth, whose name filled all mouths with envy or with praise, and he felt . . . uncertain. How to present his true account?

The President was not the only person, he told himself, filling journals with the illusion of insight through those long winter nights. Marcus Aurelius had done it before him, but Matt had the advantage of knowing that no matter what he wrote—even blabber—he could sell on retirement for fifteen or twenty million dollars. He was not a saint, by any means. Greed spurred him on; and vanity (he mocked himself) insinuated that much of what he wrote was wise, though doubtless it had all been thought or said before by lesser men or women, and phrased more simply too.

None of his thoughts, indeed, was worth the paper it was scribbled on with those bold, furious, frantic strokes; for none was reread, revised, cut, edited, reviewed. A torrent of words poured out of him, poor helpless words.

Poor madman, writing in his room.

When he was not writing, he read. Emily, the wife of the mining magnate, had sent him a parcel of books. Thomas Merton and Evelyn Underhill and Burke and Gurdjieff and many others whose names were not as widely known.

His work in the presidential office suffered; his assistants caught his mood. He was delegating more and more, and now a sense of uncertainty pervaded the halls. No one at the rudder of the ship of state.

Jim Sierra watched in horror, not knowing what was going on. His temper frayed. He snapped at his secretary, savaged a transportation paper, the product of eight months' work, and sent the Border Treaty back.

He worked relentlessly. It was not only the President's brooding that affected Jim, but the disintegration of his marriage. To forget, he threw himself into work. Sometimes, prowling late at night, he would unlock the office of an insubordinate and start in on the papers on that desk. He left complaining memos on Matt's desk about how these others were failing in their tasks.

As weeks passed, he grew openly vicious. Pete Ferrante, one personal assistant, wrote him a memo suggesting how to make an administrative procedure more efficient. Jim rocked back in his big leather chair, one foot propped casually on the desktop, and waved the young man in to wait. Pete was new in his job. He would have preferred to leave the room while his boss took time to contemplate the plan. His palms broke out in sweat. The memo was only three paragraphs long. Jim read it in one glance, stared at the boy, and slowly, with the deliberation of a mime, tore the paper top to bottom, opened his fingers and let the pieces flutter to the floor.

Then he motioned to the door. The young man went red, eyes bulging slightly, and swiveled on his heel. "Pete," said Jim. He turned back. Jim gestured to the papers on the floor. "Take that trash out as you leave."

The women in the outer office spent more time than usual in the bathroom in those days, often in tears.

Jim assumed that he was right and the universe was wrong. He surrounded himself with a kind of righteousness that is often the mark of frustration and anxiety. So, while the President was cogitating about God and nature and man's relationship to both, Jim was transferring his anger and hatred, his sense of powerlessness, onto the Eastern Orthodox. He saw in the Enemy all his own unrecognized worst traits: It was untrustworthy, violent, vengeful, and tyrannical. The only thing Jim did not notice was its fear, the mirror of his own.

Jim advocated the Ring of Fire. He believed in military control. He had only the dimmest idea that the Eastern and American Empires were allies, in un-spoken collusion, each tied to the other as strongly as combative marital partners.

The President wrote pages on such abstractions as Justice, Honor, and Patriotism. To the list, he added Freedom, Fascism, Nationalism, Communism, Capitalism, and God. In the names of these ideals, colossal crimes had been committed.

He decided these great words—Justice and Honor—were less significant than the urge that sparked them, the longing to sacrifice oneself to a higher cause. They represented no purpose other than our blind human efforts to find purpose; and the attempt itself, the energy of sacrifice, was the important thing.

Sacrifice. From *sacer* and *ficare*: to make holy.

He wondered if humans had an innate need to give themselves away, and if so, how this possibly contributed to the survival of the species. The more he considered the matter, the more he thought that the finest was often found in the lowliest activities of humankind. Little things of no importance to the world had the power to lift us to our highest moments; like the semen on Lucy's dress, and his little son's moist, hot, blond hair on the pillow as he called out, "Daddy? Daddy?" He recalled his pain the night his mother died, and the feeling of being intensely alive during the war as he drank water from a canteen. That was it, the act of struggling against loneliness or loving one's child or sorrowing in sympathy with another's grief or helping a stranger to find the way—such events put to shame the work on the Border Treaty or the purchase of new multibillion-dollar subs that could swim for three years without once surfacing for air.

So, how could humans sacrifice to a high ideal when the highest was most ordinary, when the lowest was what gave us pleasure now?

Desire lay at the root of suffering, he wrote one night; and you must not laugh, for he had never read the Buddha and did not know how ancient was the thought. If men and women could eliminate desire (attachment to desire, was what the Buddha said), then they could eliminate much pain. But how? How could he no longer care? Another night he wrote in derision of that restless, willful, self-pitying, small, crawling *I* that sets itself at the center of the universe without regard for others, demanding adoration, without humility or gratitude. It was the willful *I* that kept desiring; yet it was this *I* that also longed for its own extinction and attempted the task, one way or another, with death-defying feats of adventure (throwing oneself out of airplanes with light parachutes, or sailing single-handed across the seas), or else in destructive escapades with drugs and drink and sex, or sometimes by violent sacrifice to the famous Higher Cause (Justice, Honor, Freedom, Country, Party, and Revenge), which always—always?—led to war.

And so he wrote, trying to work out further this tenuous idea that the mystical yearning for Something Larger was no more than the ego's death-desire—when suddenly he was overpowered by the very transcendence he sought to ridicule. He was caught in a transport of feeling that had nothing to do with any love he had known before—brief sexual affairs, or the passion of romance—and trembling, he saw the perfection and the orderliness of man's killing for Honor, Justice, or Law—or *not* doing so. Killer or killed, tyrant or victim, each participated in the perfect dance. For suddenly he knew (had he not seen it already?) *there is no death.*

At that moment his heart was filled with such gratitude for life, for man, for this little planet Earth with its silver moon sailing round and round it, that he thought his bones might break. He was filled with sweetness. He loved the beggar who had been lost, and the little girl, Lily, who had brought him hope; he loved his wife, his two dead boys, and Jim's anger at his wife's desire for divorce; and all the rivals and enemies he had made in his own long climb to rule. He loved humanity with all its painful, often horrible deeds of passion and stupidity, malice, sorrow, and grief, the endless lovely strainings of heartsick humankind. He loved the desire and delusions that caused such suffering, and the fear that fueled them. He loved those flickerings of happiness that encourage and illuminate us before being replaced again by pain and loneliness and fear. And he loved the pain and terrors that led to further illumination. Poor little humankind. He loved the angel he had seen, and all the invisible spirits that he could not even imagine, but whose beneficence he felt around him at that moment. He thought of God, this Source, this creative and majestic matrix of the universe, pouring out abundance like the goddess-mother in one of his books, breasts bursting with milk, the mother-cow, gorged with milk that it pours unstinting into the mouth of its blessed suckling calf. And milk comes out in such quantity that it runs down the muzzle of the calf and smears its nose and wets its chest with its abundance. God the laughing, generous, passionate giver of all things.

Oh, he was certainly mad.

After that night he could not love enough. It was as if his heart had been opened—how? Not even by a woman's touch. And he had flown out of a cage, freed! He could not get enough of the beauties of the world— the colors, sounds!

He simply loved.

Simply he loved.

A doctor of the soul would say he was perhaps compensating for the terror of the responsibility that lay on him. For now the convoys were moving across the sands of Bessarabia and Byzantium, armies moving in cars, in tanks; and other armies were forming on the snowy passes of the Hindu Kush, where the cold was so intense you couldn't safely touch the metal of your gun; and guerrilla armies were trotting in small hungry bands through the southern jungles, furtive, full of fear, while overhead, so high they could not even be heard, planes passed screaming from day to night, carrying their fireballs.

The Ring of Fire coming.

It was the President who would give the word to begin. And now he was meeting every day with advisors about the movement of the military arms.

He wanted no responsibility for war.

Foreign ambassadors ran in and out of his office.

The war. You can't make an omelette without breaking eggs, he told himself. But he was afraid. War was in the air, and the President wondered if it was the Angel of Death that had come to him that night. He felt the fragility of life. It was all so frail.

Was that why he was swept by love?

One night, late, he padded down the carpeted hall to Anne's room. Softly he opened the door. She lay on her back in the large bed, one hand flung up as if to shield her eyes. He sat on the edge of the bed and placed his hand gently over hers. He observed in the dim light the shape of her small square fingers under his.

"Matt?"

"Don't wake up," he said.

But she shifted sleepily, bogged down in dreams. "What are you doing here? What time is it?"

"Go to sleep," he whispered. "I'm just loving you."

She mumbled something, but she was already asleep again. He stayed a few minutes more. He wanted to say a prayer, but did not know how. Time ticked by, and sitting here, half bored but unable to leave, he remembered his own mother teaching him prayers, only traces of which remained, like wisps of smoke at the back of his mind. "Our Father, who art in heaven," he began silently, not knowing what he really wanted to say anyway, until his heart found words. *Protect us all, help us all, keep us all*, he said over and over. *Protect this woman. Forgive me, Lord, for hurting her.* Then, that done, he could not stop. *Help us all, this pretty world. Help me to serve you, guide me, keep our little world, dear, loving God.*

Returning to his room, he did not remark how tenderly he had spoken to God.

The next morning Anne tracked him down at his breakfast. He sat alone at the table, the newspaper propped against a stand, reading despondent news. Anne was still in her bathrobe, her long hair loose on her shoulders, her tone of voice accusing him.

"Did you come into my room last night, at four-thirty in the morning?"

He looked up with a smile. "Four-fifteen."

She gave a laugh of disbelief. "I thought I was dreaming! Whatever were you thinking of?" She was half suspicious, half shy.

"I apologize for disturbing you." It was morning now, a different mood on him, and he didn't care about her anger anymore.

"Well you should. You did disturb me. Whatever were you in my room for anyway? People don't do that," she said. "Four in the morning. Do I have to lock my door? I don't want you in my room," she blurted.

He looked up at her. He had not noticed before how her eyelids drooped. The skin on her neck was crepey. She was getting old. He was getting old as well.

"I started thinking how much you've given me," he said. "I wanted to say thank you."

She gave him a sharp, puzzled, querying look. "Well!" Then dropped her eyes to the table. "Don't eat too much butter. It's bad for the heart. Well." She stopped uncertainly at the door to look back at him, started to speak, changed her mind and went out. The President turned back to the papers, his responsibilities, the Ring of Fire, the offensive his staff proposed.

12

For a month he did nothing about Lily. The country lay encased in snow, but the Barbarians had occupied neutral territory, and it was war that occupied the thoughts of everyone. In space the Ring of Fire turned obediently, recording with little clicks and clacks the miniature movements of toy armaments far below. And were they silent, these clicking shutters, the computer counters, when there was no atmosphere to carry sound and no one in the vacuum of space to hear?

The President had no time now for luxurious reflection. He was pulled from one conference to the next, and when he was not in meetings or making speeches—either aggressive and warning, or placa-

ting and negotiating—when he was not posing for
the photographers on the steps of the White House
with Important Men or waving from the helicopter
steps, displaying the appropriate mood of the
moment—serious or lighthearted, concerned or
victorious—when he was not reading reports or giving orders, snatching a sandwich on the run, then he
threw himself in bed, exhausted, forgetting even to
be afraid.

This was not a time to think of children or beg-
gars. The homeless no longer occupied his mind, but
the armies of the dispossessed, which swept in waves,
on foot, in carts, in cars, in horse-drawn, ox-drawn,
dog-drawn wagons, on bicycles, and on camels. Many
carried their possessions, their children, their favorite
cat or bird in their arms, and they were followed by
their dogs. People, moving in mass migrations,
searching for safety; and starvation was imminent.

We have seen this before. Every generation has
seen this anabasis accompanied by rape and pillage,
brutality, bold daylight beatings, thirst, hunger, theft.

The center would not hold.

One night the President woke up shouting in his
sleep.

Again Frank came in, and found him shaken, irri-
table.

"Just a dream. I was dreaming," he said, and returned to his nightmares.

That morning he found he could hardly get out of

bed. His legs went weak. His head was spinning. Frank helped him back to bed.

"You have a fever."

"I feel awful."

"Flu. I'll get the thermometer. Stay there," said the faithful Frank, and when he returned, the Presidential Palace scurried with calls to the doctor and trays of tea and toast. The President was exhausted. He slept one full day. His doctor ordered rest.

It was while he was recuperating that he remembered Lily. He telephoned Jake.

"I want to talk to your little girl," he said. "I want to ask her what she saw."

"She was overwrought, Mr. President. It wasn't true."

"Oh." He was disappointed. "You don't think she saw anything?"

"I know she didn't. Is it true we're sending troops to Norway?"

"I have no comment," said Matt, pure reflex. "You're out of order with that question. Anyway, I'd like to talk to her."

"No sir, I can't allow that. I won't do that to her."

"Do what?"

"Encourage her imagination. Swell her head."

"What?"

"Make her think she's special. I won't do that."

"What would it take to make you change your mind?"

That's how they negotiated. That's how the Presi-

dent arranged the small party to his Adirondack retreat for a weekend of winter sport. He needed a few
days to recuperate anyway, to get away from war. The
President asked Jim and his wife Susan (their marriage still rocking weakly along), and their children,
because this would be an informal family affair. He
invited the mining magnate, Mr. Stanhill (a major
contributor), and his wife Emily, because he wanted
to talk further with the elderly woman who had been
sending him books. He invited a speechwriter's family, and a senator, an under secretary who had teenagers, and a retired general of vast reputation, as well
as the Secretary of the Interior, who could help Jim
work the Senator over regarding the Food and Marketing Surplus Act; and finally he invited Jake and
his daughter Lily, who would enjoy herself, you see,
with the other children there. His wife, the First
Lady, had other engagements and excused herself
with graceful scented notes and spring flowers in the
rooms of every guest.

A reporter is too low on the social scale to spend
a weekend with the President, even if he covers the
White House. Jake's ambition trapped him: the
honor of the invitation, the chance to get an inside
scoop. It was understood he would not write anything that happened there, but he could use whatever he learned for "background."

The staff prepared for guests. There was to be
tobogganing and ice skating and cross-country skiing,
and, for those who liked to be indoors, there were

billiards, or bridge, or mystery novels, or talk before a blazing fire. There was food: huge breakfasts set out on the two rough sideboards—grits, eggs and bacon and sausage, chicken livers and scalloped apples, and waffles and pancakes, biscuits and butter and honey, and several kinds of jams; coffee and teas; then mid-morning snacks, and later lunch, which was also a serve-yourself picnic laid out, like breakfast, on the sideboards. Dinner each night was seated, with various courses to appeal to healthy appetites.

Jake brought Lily, but he had warned her as they drove up in his decaying Plymouth not to speak of the angel she thought she'd seen.

"Did see," she said.

"Okay." He shrugged, in no mood to dispute the point.

They drove through security checkpoints on a long and winding driveway and came to a group of rustic-looking buildings, covered with snow. Jake could imagine Jim Sierra inside, busy controlling the communications network, talking on three phones at once, smoothing over, patching up, doing in, putting out, sounding off. For this so-called "retreat" was a nerve center of power once the President arrived. At the door, Jake admonished Lily again: "I want you to have a good time. Just be careful. Remember your manners. Be on your best behavior." Lily rolled her eyes to the open sky. "Don't talk about you-know-what."

But she had no intention of talking about it.

That was why, when the President greeted her in the lodge, she shied off like a skittish deer. He frowned and drummed two fingers imperceptibly on his thumb.

That evening, the group convened for dinner, grown-ups at one table and the youngsters at another in another room, and the President made no effort to approach the little girl. But he observed with amusement how Jim's wife, Susan, seated next to Jake, bent her head toward him as he talked. She crumbled bread pills on the white tablecloth, staring intently at the table, hardly looking at him.

It was a queer match, he thought, and glanced at Jim to see his reaction; but Jim was busy with the Senator, and the Senator with the General, and later, after dinner, Jake joined them too, and their discussion of political affairs.

After lunch next day, while her father was away, Matt approached Lily for the second time.

There is nothing like a child to make a grown man feel inadequate. Lily and Jim's kids were building a snowman. Matt joined the game, although the children felt uneasy at the intrusion of their host, who came with his pack of followers. These watched from varying distances according to their rank: secret service agents, bodyguards, shadows behind trees, the Under Secretary leaning on two canes. The President dropped on his knees in the snow, organizing the kids a little more than they wanted, since he couldn't contain his habit of authority. (The Under Secretary, arthritic, stayed only a short time at the pretty winter scene before hobbling back indoors; the aides remained respectfully back.) At a certain moment the President found himself hunkered on his heels, patting the snowman next to little Lily.

"I need to talk to you," he said quietly, working intently on the snowman. He did not look at her.

"No, you want to ask me about the—about what I saw," she challenged. "But I didn't see anything. Everyone wants to ask me about that."

"You didn't?" He was disappointed. "You didn't see anything?"

"Daddy says I'm not to talk to you," she said. "Go away."

"But it belonged to *me*," he whispered back. "I have a right to know. It was *my* angel you saw!" He glared at Jim's two daughters, who had stopped their work to listen in surprise at his vehemence. "I need to know. What did it look like?" What he wanted to know was whether it looked like the ones he'd seen. Was it friendly or fierce?

"No."

He caught her tiny wrist. "Lily, wait." Then to the other two: "Why don't you two go inside?" His voice was soft. "I need to talk alone to Lily. Go along. Desmond will get you anything you want. There are marshmallows you can roast over the fire. Do you want to see a movie?" He knew children's ways.

It was an order, though. The smile did not light his eyes. The children scampered back to the main cabin at a frightened run. From the trees the secret service observed their President kneeling beside the little girl in a red snowsuit. He patted the snowman's body into shape.

"I saw an angel once," he confided. "I wonder if yours was the same."

Lily darted a suspicious look at him.

"She was very beautiful," said Matt. "I think of it as 'her.' All radiant colors. And brilliant white." The sun glittered on the snow. An icicle, hanging from the gutter of the house nearby, flashed iridescent in the sun. Lily said nothing.

"Did yours say anything? Did it tell you anything?" he asked.

"I know it was an angel," said Lily defiantly. "It was so beautiful! It was the most beautiful of anything I've ever seen." The words came tumbling from her lips so fast he could hardly keep up. "It was huge. It filled up the whole room right up to the ceiling. Only it was actually only in that one side of it, that corner, and it was all kinds of colors, shimmering. It didn't have no wings."

"Mine didn't speak," said Matt humbly, and he found his heart was beating too fast. "Did yours? Did it say anything?" Something for me, he wanted to ask.

She patted the snowman with both hands, concentrating on her task, and then suddenly turned to him, as if she had made up her mind. "Now," she said definitively, as if she had reached a decision, taken him into her confidence: "You mustn't tell. Promise?" And she smiled flirtatiously, sharing secrets, the delight of little girls. He nodded quietly.

"It waved to me," she said. "But it was so sad. I just wanted to stand there with it, that was all, and comfort it. Because it was so sad. Just the way it looked at me. Like this," she continued, attempting the expression. "It was looking that way at everyone. As if it wanted to cry. And then I waved to it, and that's when it smiled."

"Did it have a message for me?" he asked, and this time his voice cracked.

She stared at him, a guileless child. "It said, 'Don't be afraid.' And I wasn't. I wasn't afraid at all. Then the others came."

"The others?"

"Lean down," Lily whispered, and when the President bent down, she cupped her mouth to his ear with one red-mittened hand, talking confidentially. "I didn't tell anyone. Except Daddy. First there was the big one, looking so sad, and after she said, 'Don't be afraid,' that's when the singing began, like a big crowd. That was the singing you could hear. Could you hear it? There was singing everywhere, and then the angel disappeared."

Matt looked at her. It said, Don't be afraid. But were those words for him? He wanted to cry out in frustration.

She nodded solemnly. "And it was an angel. And you can't say I didn't see it, 'cause I did!"

"I know you did," he said. "That's why I need to know if the angel is always there, invisible to us, or whether it comes and goes at special times. And was it saying 'Don't be afraid' to you, or did it mean for all of us? For me? I wish I could see the angel," he confessed.

Lily stared at him thoughtfully. "Why don't you ask?"

"Ask what?"

"Ask to see it," she said seriously. "It will come if you ask." Matt broke out laughing at her childish innocence.

At this moment the photographers arrived, alert to a good picture when they saw one. Jim's two daughters were called back outside (the Under Secretary's teenagers and the Speechwriter were off skiing), and the photo of the President romping with three children in the snow appeared in every newspaper in the country.

Meanwhile, Jim's wife, Susan, was skiing along the gentle rolling golf course. Her legs and shoulders moved in ceaseless rhythm, hands reaching forward on her poles, her skis hissing in the snow. She was following, mesmerized, the flat, strong shoulders of Jake, their easy rotation, and the dark snake of his tracks unwinding from his skis before her. She thought she had never been so happy, though she could not imagine why. She wished he would stop and look at her, pause for a time and talk.

Jake slid on through the blue-gray light. He set his

concentration on the thrust of his knees, the lift of his heel in the shoe, as he tried for smoother and more rhythmical strides. He was acutely aware of the woman behind him, and decided that at the holly tree up ahead he would stop. It was a pleasure to him to impose on himself the discipline and anticipation of waiting; he could not stop until he reached the holly. He attributed to exercise his pleasure with himself, his delight in the glittering snow, the cold air scalding his nostrils at each breath, the soft shooshing of his running skis, the tense silence of the snow. Soon, though he did not know it, he would kiss her, and tilt the course of world events.

The President was at that very moment smiling his engaging grin into the camera's eye, his head thrown back with laughter, and the children pelting him with snowballs.

The Stanhills were walking hand in hand by the frozen lake, still affectionate after forty-five years of marriage. It would be nice to have a photograph of them at that moment too. And if we had one of Jim Sierra, it would be indoors as he poured whiskey in a glass, preparing to buttonhole the Senator and impress upon the poor trapped man the need to organize votes for the Farm and Marketing Surplus Act, and what benefits would accrue to the Senator if he voted right and helped the President out.

Later, over cocktails by the fire, the President snagged Jake. "I was talking to your daughter," he said amiably, and remarked the curious tensing of Jake's jaw.

"What did she say?"

"She said to ask," said Matt.

"What?"

"Nothing." He laughed. "She had her picture taken. She's a fine little girl. You're a lucky man."

"If my stupid ex doesn't spoil her," said Jake, who naturally preferred the negative.

"Oh. Do you want custody?"

"I can't take custody. I don't have time. I'm just worried the woman isn't taking care of her. I only see Lily every other weekend, so I don't get a lot of time to spend with her. I don't think her mother's feeding her right. I've told her so. She doesn't listen."

Susan joined them, smiling over the lip of her glass at Jake, who turned to include her warmly. (The President remarked it all.) Across the room, Jim was on the phone trying to control the pacing of the treaty negotiations. It would be another day before it registered on him why his wife's eyes were shining, and another day after that—back in the White House—before the rage that consumed him led him to close the borders between the two countries, the treaty quashed. He was chief of Domestic Affairs, but not afraid of extending his frontiers.

But none of that had happened yet—not the kiss Jim interrupted the following day, not the bellowing fistfight that broke out between himself and Jake, while his screaming wife tried to separate the two.

Not Jim's threats to kill Jake if he saw him again, and Jake's to lay off him, that Jim couldn't tell him what to do—no, nor Jake and Lily's hurried departure from the camp, nor Jim and Susan's long, silent, sulking drive in the station wagon back to their house from the airport, with the children feigning sleep in the back, nor Jim's subsequent terrifying collapse. For the moment, Matt lounged gracefully before the fire with Jake and Susan. He rested his elbow on the stone mantel and, for those precious moments, he forgot the war and his responsibilities. They were joined a moment later by the elegant Emily Stanhill, and then by the Under Secretary, who lowered himself into a chair from his canes.

The President looked around the comfortable room at the antlers over the fireplace, at the rough and rustic furniture, and felt a wave of inordinate fondness for this place, for these people, each driven by their virtues and vices. The Senator was absorbed by a consuming need to be reelected, and the Speechwriter burdened with the depression that had haunted him since childhood, and Jim by his need to control. Matt, in his newfound calm detachment, was amused to see that Susan had chosen for a lover her husband in a different guise. The two men did not look alike, but Jake was motivated by the same high-octane energy as Jim. Both were angry, both determined to set the world to rights. Jim's rival was his emotional twin.

At dinner the President made a joke of having no desire for peace.

"It would be a tragedy," he laughed, looking around at his guests, entertaining them with his flippancy, "to have no war. People love to make war. It staves off boredom. Listen: Of men and arms I sing! Look at the Turks and Greeks, the English and Irish, the Jews and Arabs—excuse me, Stanhill, but they love to fight. They've been fighting each other for all of recorded time. They'd feel deprived if they couldn't fight."

The group erupted in dissent.

"When I was little," said the President, "there was a man who raised fighting cocks down the street from me. Completely illegal, of course, but he used to throw his cages in the back of his car and take off for Arizona or Florida or Chicago or Georgia—all clandestine fights. He'd bet twenty thousand dollars on a single cock. He claimed he was doing them a favor, that it would be cruelty to the animals to deprive them of a fight, when that's all they wanted to do."

"Are you saying humans are like fighting cocks?" asked the Senator.

"I'm just saying we'd be doing a disservice," teased the President, "if we didn't encourage certain groups to fight. What would they do with themselves? Imagine! No war. No glory. No heroism. No literature. No purpose in life. No sorrowing over wasted lives, no men cut down in their prime—which is a mother's greatest boon, undoubtedly."

He was in prickly high spirits, explaining the need for Sacrifice to Freedom, Justice, Honor, Truth; and you could say it was in damned bad taste. "Disgusting!" Jake murmured to Susan.

"I've become cynical," Matt said to Emily, and he passed one hand across his eyes, a gesture that had become habitual now.

"The trouble is, you're not," she answered, lifting her chin with the sparkling flirtatiousness that had marked her as a twenty-year-old.

"Everyone wants peace," he said in a low voice, privately to her. "And look around the table. How many have it in their hearts? They want it on their terms, beating the enemy to a pulp, which isn't peace at all, now is it? And I'm expected to impose world peace. Let them fight, I say." They rose from the table and adjourned to the poker room, where another fire blazed.

Never again would all these people be gathered in one place. For the moment, however, one flicker in time, the members of this party challenged one another to billiards, or sat around the fire and talked, or played cards, or strolled on the squeaking snow under a cold, pale, passionate moon. And each heart held the world in microcosm, each moment held in it a teardrop of eternity. Yet none of them knew it. Not a person there, unless it was the lovely, elderly Emily, guessed that in his or her own hands hung the totality of life and time. Not a single one of them except perhaps the President, who was still groping toward the understanding, guessed the secret: that we get to choose our lives—not what happens to us, necessarily, but how much we see. We get to choose our responses—whether to be enslaved by desires and fears, or to let go, to trust, to take life's dare, and in that willingness to experience, if only for the briefest moment, the release that comes with the opening of the heart.

The other part of the secret is how hard it is to do this, how much practice it takes to make it into a habit, so that we are no longer held hostage by our instincts. There's no harder struggle in the world. But it's there to be chosen if we wish.

So, everything was going as it should. The world was burning up with joy and love, with anger and grief, with creation and destruction, and the people who were gathered on that weekend were burning with their own desires and delusions, hatred, fears, and love.

They say that to talk of love is to make love. All that night Emily Stanhill and the President danced a conversational minuet around the meaning of evil and the nature of God. For Emily, to talk of God was to talk of love, and Matt could not help but be moved. She described to him how to pray in such a way that your prayer is heard and answered. "It's a law," she said, "a simple, esoteric exercise. It's what Christ was talking about, and it's rarely taught in

church. But done that way, it's always answered."
(And he would remember this conversation much
later, when she was dying of cancer and asked him
for his prayers.)

"But you have to ask," she said, echoing the words
of the little child, "otherwise the help can't come."
He was struck by the coincidence of hearing this direction twice in the same day, once from a five-year-
old, and once from a woman of seventy-two. "And
finally, after making your request, ask for the Highest
Good for all concerned, say thank you, and be willing to let go."

"Be willing not to get the prayer?" He laughed. "I
thought you said it was always answered."

The fire dimmed. The other guests joined them at
times, contributing snatches of poetry or their own
noisy beliefs, and Emily observed (laughing to the
President) that each person considered his opinion as
the One True Word. Each one thought that he (or
she) was right and the others mistaken or misin-
formed.

Her husband, the mining magnate, went to bed.
The children had long before gone up. The others
followed, trailing off in twos and threes or one by
one. Emily danced a fox-trot with the President to
the radio, then a stately and old-fashioned waltz. Susan and Jake came inside from their moonlight walk,
blowing on their fingers and casting lingering side-
long looks at one another; they could hardly break
apart, and walked upstairs to their respective rooms,

shoulders brushing like butterflies, leaving the President and Emily alone, still talking on the couch.

He confided in her. He told her about the angels in his bedroom (first compassionate, then angry), and about the beggar. What did it mean? He spoke haltingly at first, anticipating ridicule. Instead she listened, nodding as if his story were as natural as pine trees, and once she gave a startled exclamation of delight. He told of his confusion, his longing for solitude, his boredom with much of what he had to do, his obsession with the angel, the vagrant, the desperate wilderness he was in.

"Dark night," she murmured.

"What?"

"Dark Night of the Soul. St. John of the Cross."

"I don't know about that," he said stiffly, a little annoyed at not being found more special. He didn't want just a common, everyday mystical experience. She laughed.

"It's all right, Matt. Every single person is unique. Isn't that a miracle? And each experience of God is utterly unique. Yet, still, we all follow a similar path. You are so lucky."

"Yes?"

"To have this anguish. It means your shell is cracking. It's going to be wonderful, Matt."

"Yes?"

"Yes," she repeated. "You should give thanks for this gift. God is reeling you in like a fish. But you have to go through the darkness before you find the light. It's going to be wonderful."

"I don't even know if what I saw was real."

"No. You'll only know by its effects."

"What do you mean?"

"By whether you change, and how the new knowledge is manifested in your life."

She actually spoke like that, and he thought, listening to her lilting sweet voice, that he had never heard such lovely turns of phrase. He didn't laugh.

"But what's wrong with me?" he asked. "I'm raw feeling. I look at the simplest thing—two lovers," he added, these being the last objects he had noticed, "and tears well up in my eyes. I can't control myself."

She said very little. Nodded. Mmm. Simply talking to her made the President feel better.

"So, then, do you go to church?" he asked, interested.

"No. But I believe in God. I have had experiences of my own. I guess many people have. And, yes, I believe you, first because I've seen some of what you're describing, secondly—because I believe you, that's all. Only you need a guide. You can't take this journey without a spiritual guide."

"What journey?"

"The spiritual journey. To your soul. Who was it who said that when you find your Self you find God? Was it Jung? That's what's coming to you."

"God?"

"God. The Self. Once your soul catches fire, once

it has seen into that other dimension, you can't put the fire out. It'll never be the same again. That's all that's happening. It's not extraordinary."

"It is," he said stubbornly.

"Well, I mean no more than the other miracles around us: like a tulip or a terrier dog. Or the constant recurrence of love. Those are miracles!" She laughed.

Later, at the end of the evening, when they traced their steps to their respective rooms, she kissed his cheek good night; or morning, for it was three A.M.

"Good night, Emily."

"Good night, Mr. President. God bless you."

"He has. I hope He has."

Then he entered the room and went on his knees beside his bed as she had directed and said his prayers. Innocently. Like a child.

13

"**A**dulteress!" hissed Jim as they drove home from the airport. His voice was low so the children, in the back of the station wagon, would not hear. Susan flinched.

"Adulteress," he repeated. "Assassin. You have assassinated our marriage."

"Fuck off," she said.

It was the adultery that overwhelmed him; he had a sudden memory of himself at the age of ten, watching from the third floor of the embassy in Rome—his beautiful mother in a black velvet evening gown, his father with his strong moustache. They faced each other on the staircase below him; and he, Jimmy, held the banister posts as if in a cage and pressed his face to the slats, listening, wide-eyed, as his father shouted to her: "Shame!"

"Shame!" Jim cried, to clear his mind. "I'll see you get nothing out of this," he threatened Susan. "Not one penny. Not the house. Not the children."

"They're my children too." She spoke through gritted teeth, voice low, not to wake them. "My house."

Then the appalling silence.

"Don't drive like a maniac," said Susan. "Slow down."

In the backseat the children exchanged frightened looks and curled into the pretense of sleep.

That night she called Jake on the downstairs phone.

"I have to see you."

"Now?"

"No, no. I can't come now. But, oh Jake, talk to me. He called me an adulteress. He wants the children."

"Are you afraid of him?"

"He's been violent before," she whispered into the phone, listening for his step. "Tomorrow. Can I see you tomorrow?"

So they made their assignation, exchanged their lovers' vows and waited, lunging between ecstasy and despair, which is the condition of humankind in the grip of love or war.

Jim had declared war against Jake, and his anger extended to the President, who was shilly-shallying about war, and the Barbarian Empire.

The story of war is always the same. It is a strategy, a chess game of how to kill without being killed. Feed Jake lies. Let him print part truths which Jim would then correct; let Jake get bombed—egg on his face—kill his reputation. It was a vicious, secret, covert war that Jim led, unannounced, but no less real for that.

Jim put his attention to it with all the brilliance of his law school career. A word dropped to an aide—a leak suggested—a little packet of poisoned meat thrown out from the sleigh onto the snow behind. A cautious war. No one must trace it back to him, because if the source were known, the running wolf would pass the bait. While thinking of animals, Jim decided he could kill two birds with one stone, disgrace Jake and push his own idea of a foreign policy. The stories he was foisting onto Jake were of Matt's increasing thrust toward war. The President was held in check only by his military advisors. It was easy for Jake to believe it: Hadn't he heard the President teasing at dinner at the Adirondack retreat?

That was how Jim set up Jake, the lover of his adulteress wife.

And meanwhile Jim still sneaked at night into other people's offices, read their memos, answered the mail, signed their signatures, burying himself in work, to keep from thinking of the adulteress back home; and if Susan screamed at him at night, locked him out of the bedroom, while he pounded furiously on the door, if the neighbors woke from the noise of their quarreling, and the children crouched in their beds, hugging each other in tears, he felt justified in the fact that it was all her fault. He refused to give her a divorce. She refused to leave the house. She insisted it was hers as much as his, and twice she changed the locks, so that he had to break a window to get inside (the same one twice).

He drank a lot.

Meanwhile, Matt's condition did not go unnoticed. Jim was concerned enough to convene a secret meeting of advisors, after which a series of small meetings with two members of the military and Chief of Staff, with Steven Dirk and a senator from Wyoming, and the Majority Leader of the House. A secret conclave, respectfully considering the removal of the President. There was cause for concern. The President had gone sour on the job.

Perhaps he had. By much care, Matt had managed to extricate himself from certain duties, so that every day after lunch he stole time for himself, but this time was not productively spent in athletics or games, in chasing women or tasting wines or in reading history or government reports. It was spent doing nothing. That's what Jim found disconcerting. The President sat on the White House balcony, wrapped in a blanket against the chilly weather, and gazed unseeing across the lawn to the Washington Monument and thence to the Jefferson Memorial. Or he sprawled in a chair in his private rooms and stared at the fire in the hearth. Forty minutes later Frank would knock discreetly, bringing him a demitasse of espresso or a hot China tea in a Limoges cup. Then the President's day would begin again, rushing to ceremonies, meetings, photo sessions, and more meetings with advisors, with congressmen or senators, with members of his cabinet, with lobbyists and constituents, conferences over breakfast, over cocktails, over dinners, and more ceremonious events and formal appearances at theaters or concerts at which, being President, he never got to stay to the end.

To an outsider observing him on the balcony, wrapped in his blankets (the secret service nightmare), he might have appeared to be brooding darkly. Actually, he was praying for God's will.

This is what Emily had told him about prayer:

Imagine there's a dog that is attacked by a pack of wild dogs, tearing and biting. The dog manages to pull away and run for its life. Limping, it drags itself home and drops at its master's feet. What does it do? It cannot speak. It can only look miserably at its owner, whine, beat its tail in the dust. And what does the man do? He picks up the dog, takes it inside, washes and bandages its wounds and gives it food and water, antibiotics, a warm bed to sleep on, maybe some brandy down its throat. He takes it to the vet. Every day he changes the dressings, and soon the dog is well.

The dog has asked for none of these things. All it did was to present itself and beat its tail in the dust.

That (said Emily) is how you pray to God. Because if you ask for a shirt, you will get a shirt, and if you ask for a pair of pants, you will get a pair of pants. But if you merely present yourself, then God will give you . . . everything.

"That's how you pray," she'd said. "You ask to know God's will."

"I can't do that," he had muttered.

"Then pretend."

So he prayed, black dog.

I said he found decisions hard, lives hanging in the balance. He comforted himself that his intentions were good, that purity of intent sufficed. But did it? Slyly, he asked advice. Sometimes he ignored the counsel once given, and made no decisions, but meekly deferred to the nonaction that was a form of action too, the decision to do nothing. Other times he took the advice of the majority, or sometimes of the counselor he liked best, independent of political consideration.

Sometimes, in private, behind closed doors, he flipped a coin. Or he took a pack of cards and turned up two (or three), the high card being winner (or the red, or the diamond of the suit).

There were people who thought the country was never better run than during this time when, going mad, the President left decisions to the angels with the flip of a coin. His wisdom was praised, especially by those whose advice he took. But he was walking on eggshells all the time.

Did he know the party was divided into factions, waiting for his mistake?

Meanwhile other items hit the Press: a famine below the Equator, an earthquake in Turkey, a typhoon that wiped out two Pacific islands. Attention focused on finding food for refugees. Little wars broke forth and were stamped out like brushfires.

And then there were the personal cruelties inflicted by ignorance or mistake, and these flared truer, brighter, for being isolated horrors of abnormal moment, and not all of them were crimes.

A Montana man murdered his two daughters and fed them to his pigs. He was judged insane.

A son shot both of his violent and abusive parents with a double-barreled .20-gauge. He was charged with murder.

A runaway girl, only fourteen years old, telephoned her mother, begging to come home. "I want to come home," she sobbed, and the way she hovered on the word *home*, holding the sound in her mouth, spoke of her yearning. Her mother told her no, she'd found a man she was living with and he wouldn't put up with a child. "Mom, I want to come home!" A pimp took her in and treated her relatively decently, meaning he beat her only when he could not afford his drugs. The girl was picked up by the police and jailed dozens of times. Her mother was never charged with any crime.

Oh, there were many things to occupy our minds, lawsuits and taxes and diseases and eighteen-year-old sons who left college to play the guitar as traveling minstrels; and the family men who engaged their little daughters in sex. One of these was a violinist who accosted his niece from the ages of nine to fourteen, and afterward went to the symphony hall, where he played like Orpheus. Women wept at his rendition of Beethoven's violin concerto. So emotionally removed was he from his acts that when, at fifteen, his niece slashed her wrists, it never crossed his mind that his gifted hand had held her knife. He played at her funeral so poignantly that everyone agreed his powers were increasing with every passing year.

Pain lay everywhere. There were vandals and street gangs shooting themselves with dope or their enemies with guns, and terrorist bands that took hostages for ransom or threw bombs, sublimating their helpless rage into political acts, and feeling nobler, thereby, than the common rapist or gangster; and in almost every country of the world there were secret police who were paid by their governments to inform against the very people whom they served.

Just as you despaired, you saw babies were born in all the colors and tones of the earth, each with their tiny fairy fingernails and lungs like a blacksmith's bellows. There were heroes in hospitals returning the dead to life, and heroines battling against disease and common folk who merely held out daily hands to one another, giving heart.

Yes, the world was a fascinating place in which to live in those years, and not much different than in other periods, though it was burning up. No one, man or woman, had learned to eliminate anger from his heart. Or loneliness. Or jealousy. Or any of the excesses of compulsive desire. So everything continued burning up.

Like Jim. Like Susan. Like Jake. Like the President himself, burning up with longing to see God.

14

This is the story of a spiritual experience and the dismantling of a man of power. Did it happen in this way? It always does. This is not a unique event. It happens all the time, though not usually so dramatically as with an angel at your bed.

Nonetheless, thousands, maybe millions, of people reach a moment in their lives and are shown ... what? What cannot be spoken of, and so they don't. Many hesitate even to share it with their best beloved friends, perhaps especially not with them, not with mother or father or husband or wife or lover or close friend. For one thing, what is there to tell? That for a moment a curtain fell before their eyes, exposing them to light? Or to knowledge they have no language to describe? Sometimes this experience comes soft as mist, curling slowly into consciousness over many years, seeping through the chinks in their protective doors until they are filled, though there is no single event with which they mark a revelation. Grace. To others it comes as glimmers in the night, half discerned from the corner of an eye and gone when they turn their head to look—except, with a shudder, they realize that in that moment everything has changed. The world is no longer as before. They are different, though they cannot say how or what exactly is new, unless it is a kind of lightheartedness, a luminous equanimity that they carry with them even in distress.

To still others, this knowledge comes bowling over them in a vision or a voice—Epiphany!—Moses on the mountaintop, the burning bush and all that. It tears the blinkers of the material world from their eyes, cracks open consciousness. Some go mad with God-consciousness. Some are saints, and others are just ordinary people who try the patience of family and friends by talking about God, or Christ, or Allah to any stranger who sits beside them on a bus.

There are a lot of them out there.

You would think this thing, happening to so many people, would change the world. You would think that this man or that woman—become a god now, a goddess, having been given this glimpse of immortality—would trumpet it from the rooftops. *Ladies! Gen-*

*tlemen! Thieves! Clowns! Brothers, sisters mine! Listen
to what I find!*

You would think that people would hear about an
angel, or a burning bush, and tell others, and they in
turn would pass the good news on, so that whole
populations would convert. Isn't that what should
have happened when the papers printed how a little
girl had seen an angel in the Presidential Palace over
the holidays? True, some of the papers reported it as
a cute Christmas tale, a human interest story, but
with no more significance than you would give to a
recipe for cheese soufflé.

Why did readers not become inflamed with the
meaning of the news? Because they couldn't. It is
part of the Law. Oh, if you tell your dearest friend
about an angel that you saw, then she might believe.
She might believe because she would hear the soft-
ening and passion in your voice, see the trembling of
your body. She would catch your emotion and be
moved by it, and, because she knows you, she would
suspend disbelief and let her heart lift up in trust.
And if she continued, defying doubt for days, or
months, a year, her faith would be replenished by experiences of her own, so that she'd have her own stories to pass on.

But if she tried to tell the news about the angel to
a third party, the whole thing would fall flat. The angel wasn't hers, and the third person is left un-
touched.

Why is that?

I think it is to save us. It is a protection for the material system in which we live. Because the whole world would go mad with God-knowledge. People would run out into the streets laughing and dancing and throwing their arms around one another in their joy. They would stand weeping at the vision of a flowering crab-apple tree. And as for a sunset . . . can you imagine!

Everyone in the world would run outdoors on that day the News was known. Drinkers in bars, and commuters on their travels home, and lovers in each other's arms, housewives cooking dinner, and mothers feeding their little children, torturers in prisons— they would all run outdoors at once to see this miracle, the gorgeous violent choir of a sunset; and like a great hum this marvel would pass right around the world, so that an observer on another planet (if he had a strong enough telescope) might think that the scurrying of footsteps as they hurried after the view, the populations running west, was turning the globe on its axis, millions of moving feet. And a cry of wonderment would burst from every throat, a great sigh, a sound equal to the visual adoration spread before them, if they knew the News; and the cry would ripple westward all the way around the world, till it hit us in the back again at dawn.

Oh, we'd all go mad with God-knowledge. And that is why the News can only be received shyly, one-on-one.

Otherwise it would destroy the game. The game of

hide-and-seek, that is, in which each individual gets to make up the rules of whichever game he wants to play. Hide-and-seek with intellect. Or warfare. Or with fame and glory. Hide-and-seek with hunger and starvation, death and disease and grief. Jealousy, rejection, isolation. Hide-and-seek with material possessions. Or sex. Or loss. Or love. It's all one game, the hide-and-seek with God.

And what of the person, man or woman, who is smitten with God-knowledge, either glimpsed through mists or seen in revelations?

The spiritual journey is a serious pastime.

It is undertaken alone, in secret, and each person sets off, like the Pilgrim with his pack, and leaves behind (to his dismay) his family, friends, engagements. Nothing satisfies. Not music or books or art or theater. They are suddenly tasteless to one who is thirsting for the spiritual.

Then it's as if he is on a picnic with his loved ones on the side of a hill, with the city lights spread out below, and all the others in the family, the rest of the picnic, are exclaiming at the twinkling little city lights, while he sees at the top of the hill the light of the Universal Force. "Come on," he says. "Hurry. Do you see it? There! Come on!" But he cannot get their attention, because they're admiring the lesser lights of the little human city down below.

Once struck with spiritual hunger, once you set out on the Path, you are lost to the world that displays itself to others. A wise man once said that we,

Homo sapiens (so termed), are driven by four goals only, four great desires. Some people want one and some another and some want combinations of the four. In one category are all the sensual pleasures, of food and sex and silks and luxuries. Second is money, the miser storing up raw gold (or oil or real estate or art). The third is lust for fame and glory, the immortality that comes when your name rings through the corridors of history. And last is power over others. It is true that some people want knowledge, mistaking it for wisdom, and artists want desperately the conditions to create. But they want recognition too, acknowledgment, which is a form of lust, and they take bites of all the other three.

Those people on the spiritual journey, however, want none of them. Only the direct experience of God will do, of the love that moves the sun and stars.

Later, as their journey proceeds, they come back to the physical world. They get pleasure again from music or art or sensual delights, sex, status, security, and even enjoy their successes, but never again do they want power over another, and never again do they lust after personal fame or feel the need for sex or food or possessing people in the same way as before. They appear to drink from the same fountain, but the water they taste is different, infinitely sweet.

That was the state of the President, Matt Adams. He did not know yet (though Emily had said it right out loud) that he was on a path. His emotions were horses, one minute bolting in panic and the next whickering as they stepped into the first green dawn of the world. His staff noticed how often he muttered aloud. As if (Jim said with a sneer) he were talking to someone over his shoulder.

"What should I do?" he'd say, or, "What do you want me to do now?"

And still he vacillated on the war. One last time he tried to stop it. "I don't want to do it," he said openly in the middle of a strategy meeting.

There was stunned silence. The General coughed into his hand.

"It's not respectful."

"Respectful of whom, Mr. President?"

"Respectful of them. Let them have their war, I say, without—"

"We have our defenses to maintain, sir," the General explained patiently, wondering why the President didn't understand.

"They're our allies," interrupted Jim. "If we don't go in, then. . . ."

But a buzz went up in the President's head, a host of bees. He was no longer listening, for he knew the argument: if not us, them. He frowned at his laced fingers on the tabletop and tried to concentrate. Only a few nights earlier he had thrilled to the perfection of the universe, the planets swinging in their arcs, the people pursuing pleasures and pains, and it had all enchanted him. Even the suffering of life— the cruelty and violence, hunger, sickness, loneliness, humiliation—had all seemed balanced by the wealth of joys; not one terror would he have given up, not one that did not seem to have its own reward.

And now he was being swept to war. And where was God in this? Where was the perfect order of the universe?

He sat in the rich surroundings of this meeting, his hands reflected in the glossy surface of the mahogany table. Was warfare part of God's desire? Was death and killing? What about lies, destruction, famine, fear? If his armies joined the fight, did that act upset the balance of terror and constitute by the purity of his intent a good? Just as he was ready to open his mouth and ask outright—but does belligerence bring peace?

"Think of Munich, Mr. President."

"Think of Chamberlain."

He passed one hand across his eyes.

"Hitler."

"Stalin."

"Democracy."

"It's really not an option, sir. If we don't protect our interests, we lose the ... Domino ... Sikhs ... oil ... madman ... Democracy ... foothold in ... Fireball. ..." Again his mind began to buzz. Somehow he could no longer hear the words that in previous times had brought him to arms, made his heart crouch, like a tiger, tail lashing, ready to attack. A hive of bees was burrowing in his brain.

No wonder the vice-president and Jim, two members of the military, and various others felt betrayed. No wonder they were planning the coup. The President was cracking up. They could prove it. He was no longer compos mentis.

And all the while, the march of war continued, and Jim and Jake faced each other in open combat, and Susan and Jim, and the children, like refugees in their own rooms, hugged their stuffed animals and sucked their empty thumbs for sustenance.

The fact is, Jim loved his wife. He wanted her back. That was why he made life miserable for her. One day he asked her to have dinner with him.

"Why?" she asked suspiciously.

"Just to talk, for Christ's sake. Can you give a little, Susan?"

She relented guiltily. "Because he's the father of my children," she confided stiffly to her best girlfriend. "Because we've lived together thirteen years."

They went to a restaurant. Jim was determined to show her a good time, to demonstrate that she was wrong to cast him out: he, on the White House staff, a man of status, power, charity.

He shaved before he picked her up. He put on aftershave. He brought her flowers and laughed aloud when he saw his girls and opened his arms for them to run into—

"Ceci!" he called. "Ginny!" And the girls fell into his warm embrace. He picked them up and kissed their fine hair, felt their arms around his neck and knew suddenly that everything was going to be all right.

Call it intuition. Clarity. He knew with every fiber

of his body that he and Susan would be together again, one happy family, with Jake forgotten, or better yet, dead; Jim would win her back. Courtship. Another kind of war. . . .

He gave her the flowers. "You look nice," he said. "New dress?"

"No." She felt confused, because he'd seen it a dozen times over the past two years, and why was he courting her when he knew she wanted to marry Jake?

"New haircut? You look terrific."

"Jim, it's exactly the same."

He was annoyed that his gesture was not accepted.

"Well, it's very nice," he plowed on anyway. Courtship. War. "You look good. I've made reservations at . . ."

They sat at their table, Susan rolling bread pills between her fingers with intense concentration. The pills spilled out of her bread plate onto the white linen as Jim talked, and she gathered them into little piles and reorganized them into rows. Jim ordered wine at fifty-six dollars for the bottle of red: nothing too good for his wife.

He talked about himself, his hopes, the President, the political situation. He talked about Steve, who annoyed him with his nitpicking microdecisions; and about his new secretary, who could not find the simplest files; and the Border Treaty, which the Ambassador had put back on the track; and Susan still said nothing, but ate quietly, eyes on her plate, never looking in his eyes as she twirled her bread with fretful fingers. Jim grew expansive under the influence of the red, and then he told her in a lowered, intimate voice of his concerns about the President, and finally, proudly, of the coming coup.

"There's a group of us. It's all legal. We're following procedure."

"But what's he done?"

"It's what he hasn't done," cried Jim, and explained the peril of the situation. "No one knows what's the matter. He's not interested in anything. If he doesn't want to be President, he ought to step down," he said (but in a suitable whisper). Then, because now he really had her attention, he laid out the plan to her. Then he paid and got her coat from the cloakroom and put it over her shoulders politely and drove her home and parked. Then he rested his arm on the back of the seat, fingering her hair:

"Can I come in?" he asked, congratulating himself on giving her such control.

"Not tonight." She looked at her fingers. "Not tonight," she repeated and opened the door. "Thank you, Jim. It was nice."

He was surprised. "Is that all? It was nice?"

"You want more?" By now she was half out of the car. He started to grab her arm, then caught himself and opened his own door and walked around to her.

"Of course I want more," he said, following her up the walk. "I want you. I want my home and kids. I want us to be together. I got mad. I admit I haven't been the best husband, but we can make it. I know we can. If you give us a chance. We have a good marriage, Susan."

For a moment her heart opened, seeing him so boyish and appealing. Then he said: "Get rid of the guy. Promise you'll never see him again, and I'll forgive everything."

Like a box, her heart clicked shut. You could have heard it lock. She shook her head. "Good night, Jim."

"What the fuck does that mean? Wait!"

"No, I can't."

"You can't! Can't what? Can't stop screwing him? Or won't, you goddamn whore!"

The door closed in his face. In the car, Jim sat behind the wheel, blinded by his tears. His shoulders shook with sobs.

Who can say why things happen as they do? We ascribe a motive, and neglect to see the other causes there. The President had organized his winter weekend for the single purpose of talking to one little girl, five years old, and it resulted in her father's attraction to a married woman, their kiss, another link in the chain of events.

The next morning, Susan told Jake on the phone everything that happened on her date with Jim. "It was awful. There's nothing between us now. I never want to see him again." That's what she thought was important. As an aside she remembered to pass on the news about the coup.

He whistled. That's what he thought was important. "Who's in on it?"

The cat out of the bag.

"God bless you, Susan," said Jake before putting down the phone, and she was touched by both the words and the feeling with which he said them, and spent the afternoon drifting and dreaming about Jake. She took it personally. But when Jake dropped the phone onto its cradle, he took a quick turn around the desk in his excitement, for now it required only an energetic, resourceful journalist to confirm the facts and break a Pulitzer Prize–winning story on page one above the centerfold. Susan never entered his mind at all.

The question was, what to do with the information? Print it? Let the traitors know he had a leak?

"I think you should take it to the President first," said Susan a few days later.

Jake laughed. "The President!" Her innocence.

"I think he's nice," said Susan. "He sent me flowers once. I yelled at him and he sent me flowers."

"That's no reason," said Jake, shifting her head onto his shoulder. But he had softened toward Matt now that he, Jake, had authority to topple his authority.

"Also, if it weren't for him, we wouldn't have met," she said.

"Tell you what," said Jake. "I'll print it. But two hours before it's on the stands, we're going to warn him, how 'bout that? To get a reaction. I've already talked to the editors. He can avert the coup and I'll get my Pulitzer both." And he hugged her to show it was a joke.

"Jim will be fired, you know," he added.

"Let him," said Susan.

"He won't get another job easily," warned Jake. "You may have trouble getting child support."

"He's not giving it now," she said fiercely. "Let him suffer."

War.

"I love you," said Jake.

"I love you too," she said, not knowing—how could she yet?—of the misuse of her verb; that you cannot love one person and wish harm to another. It is a paradox, but at least she meant at that moment that she needed Jake. . . . What goes around comes around. Did she have any idea how her hatred would boomerang back onto herself, as war will always do?

"Let him suffer," she said fiercely, and never imagined how only days later Jim would burst into the Oval Office and sweep the President's papers on the floor, try to hit Matt, his idol, his ideal, knock over the flag in a scuffle with the staff, and then dash out of the palace and down the drive, shouting as he wound through traffic to his old home.

"Adulteress! Adulteress!" he repeated to himself, weeping as he remembered his beautiful mother bending over his dead father, and his own sense of abandonment. He wiped the tears from his angry eyes.

He found Jake in the kitchen with Susan. "Adulteress. You whore!" He took a fireplace poker and broke his house apart, in his effort to reach Jake, his wife, his very heart. Jake and Susan ran to a neighbor's house. They called the police. The children, thank God, were in school.

He tore the books from the shelves, the groceries from the kitchen cabinets, the goose down from the living room pillows, so that feathers billowed and floated through the house, merging on the upper floors with the stuffing from the huge mattress off the bed that he slashed with a knife and threw down the front stairs.

The police took Jim to a hospital for observation. Susan's house was wrecked.

That same night, as Jake and Susan lay in bed together, happy in their pillow talk and bonded by lament, the President had his final dream. In his dream the beggar approached. He was barefoot. In rags. At his side was a large black dog. The beggar held out the paperweight to Matt, who took it, at which the man changed before Matt's eyes, was clothed in waves of white so brilliant that the President had to look away.

When he turned back, the beggar was gone, but in his hand Matt held the paperweight. He turned it over and a storm of snowflakes fell over the earth, or white joy, like angels flying everywhere, and they filled the air with a song so sweet that he knew he was dreaming in the dream. He was ravished by the music in his dream.

When he awoke he knew ... everything.

15

They say that a person cannot change, but this is simply not true. He proceeds through life, and if he's successful, goes through transformations that make him more of what he was before, closer to the child; and that is what happened to the President, Matthew Madison Adams, who woke one morning to see an angel at the foot of his bed, and began, against his will, his hero's journey. His revelation came as no powerful fireworks display, bombs bursting in air, enlightenment. Rather, it took a long and gradual opening of the heart, but it was no less heroic because interior and uncoordinated and chronologically unclear. It was his own wilderness he traveled through, slaying the dragons of doubt and insecurity, blindness, egotism, control, and arrogance, slaying the numbness that masked his feelings and fear. What he learned was simply to give up.

It was a descent into Hell. But Hell is also only an attitude of mind, for Heaven is in Hell, as Jakob Böhme wrote, and Hell in Heaven, yet separated by the most immeasurable distance of our point of view.

Matt awoke from his dream (the last one he would ever have of the beggar and the angels). He took command. He held the reins of power firmly in his hands, confident once more, decisive, with a twinkle in his eye, and with a sense of timing that left both his admiring supporters and opposition in awe. His change in attitude alone was enough to abort the coup: Forget Jake's story, which, scrabbling to catch up to the swiftly changing events, was written and revised a dozen hurried times before it appeared and won the Pulitzer for Jake. By then the vice-president had dropped into line, as had the two military officers. The President was the alpha dog again, with the rest of his staff at his shoulder, looking to him for leadership, and he to his angels. He felt a promise had been made to him.

He ordered the armed forces on maneuvers, building to Operation Shark, and you could see Time holding its breath as the world moved breathlessly toward this last encounter with death. The little planet would be a Black Hole itself if Matt guessed wrong. But the President pressed on, fearful at times and often caught by doubt, but mostly feeling more excitement than anxiety, after what he'd seen. Some people were scared by the very confidence they had once found wanting.

"Do you think we get out of school so fast?" He laughed. "Not likely. Not yet."

Some people weren't sure the planet was in school, but who could resist the President? His spirit was infectious. He rode high in the polls again, unconquerable, and when he campaigned for reelection, when he addressed the roaring crowds, he was unbeatable; even Anne took to the hustings, as in the old days—Battling Annie at his side. But I'm ahead of myself again, for the landslide election did not come until years later; long after Susan's divorce from Jim, long after the armies crossed the border to challenge the Barbarians, after the Ring of Fire was ignited, then extinguished, and after the famous summit meeting that dismantled the Ring forever.

The summit took place on an ancient estate outside Stockholm, during summer days without an end to light. The President walked out with the elderly Eastern Premier, down the path through the pine forest. Only the two walked together, for the Premier spoke the President's language fluently, though Matt knew only a few words of that ancient tongue. The Premier leaned on the cane he had used since his illness the year before.

It would be a lie to say the two had forgotten enmity. They paced slowly up the path, side by side, the scent of pine in their nostrils and the soft green light splashing at their feet. The breeze rocked the branches above and gently nuzzled at their cheeks and the skin at their open shirts.

Ahead of them moved the two angels. The President blinked against the tremendous light.

"You have one too," the President said.

"It came before the war."

"Mine too." The President nodded absently. "Yours has a sword." But no sooner had he spoken than the sword of light turned into a column as large as the two haloed, mistlike figures.

"The sword of combat," growled the Premier, trying to hold on to his failing sense of animosity, and watching as the sword hilt shifted, as before, into that luminous cross.

Observers following fifty yards behind saw the two heads of state, the Emperors, who between them governed half the world, pause and stop. The Premier leaned on his cane. Both men seemed absorbed in gazing at something ahead—a squirrel perhaps? A bird?

"The sword of conflict," repeated the Premier hoarsely. But as he spoke they saw it once more change into a round and shining globe, held as tenderly as the orb in the other angel's hands. "Yours has one too." And the two spheres merged into one huge ball, held up by both these beautiful creatures.

The Premier could not stop his flowing tears, and standing in the center of the path, he found he could not move. Then he felt the President's hand on his shoulder, and, looking over, saw that he was weeping too. For angels filled the sky. Their light extended everywhere.